STORIES FROM THE UKRAINE

Mykola Khvylovy

STORIES FROM THE
ukraine

Translated
with an Introduction by
GEORGE S. N. LUCKYJ

Philosophical Library
New York

The author wishes to express appreciation to the Safe-
Way Construction Company Limited for their kind
assistance in the preparation of this publication.

Acknowledgment is made to the following, for their
kind permission to reprint: the publishers and editors of
the *Slavonic and East European Review,* for the "Puss
in Boots"; to Columbia University Press, for material
from *Literary Politics in the Soviet Ukraine*: 1917-1934;
and to editors of *Harvard Slavic Studies,* vol III.

CONTENTS

Introduction   1

PUSS IN BOOTS   15

MY SELF (ROMANTICA)   31

A SENTIMENTAL TALE   56

THE INSPECTOR-GENERAL   126

IVAN IVANOVICH   160

HIS SECRET   215

INTRODUCTION*

Mykola Khvylovy (real name Fitilov) was born on December 1, 1893. Very little is known about his early life. Although, according to Soviet sources, he came from a working class family, there are good reasons to believe that his father was a teacher in the village of Trostyanets, in the province of Kharkiv.** Khvylovy's mother, nee Elizabeth Tarasenko, was of peasant origin. Young Mykola's education was scrappy and incomplete; it did not extend beyond the fifth grade of the *gymnasia*. Although not fond of learning, he read a great deal and was deeply impressed by the works of Gogol and Shevchenko. Both these fellow countrymen of Khvylovy later influenced his artistic temperament: the first sharpened his feeling for satire, the second strengthened his patriotic zeal.

---

* I am grateful to the publishers for permission to use here material which was first included in my book *Literary Politics in the Soviet Ukraine; 1917-34* (New York, Columbia University Press, 1956) and the article "The Battle for Literature in the Soviet Ukraine: A Documentary Study of VAPLITE," *Harvard Slavic Studies*, III.

** All Ukrainian place names are transliterated here from the original.

1

Shortly before the outbreak of World War I Khvylovy tried, unsuccessfully, to earn his living as a clerk, and later as a locksmith's apprentice. In 1915 he was conscripted into the Russian army. It was during the next two years that Khvylovy became a revolutionary.

The revolution of 1917 had a different character in the Ukraine than it had in Russia. In the Ukraine it was fought primarily as a war of national liberation. United in their goal, the Ukrainians were divided as to what kind of government should prevail in their country, freed from Russian rule. While the majority of them were in favor of a sovereign republic governed by a constituent assembly, some Ukrainian political parties advocated a socialist system, similar to that proclaimed by the Russian Bolsheviks. Khvylovy sided with the minority. His revolutionary career began in 1917 when he emerged as a member of a small band of peasant insurgents led by the Ukrainian Socialist Revolutionary, Pushkar. Later Khvylovy led another peasant rebel column and early in 1919, when the forces of the democratic Ukrainian People's Republic were defeated by the Russian Red Army, he joined a Soviet military unit in the Ukraine.

The fact that Khvylovy became a communist and a party member did not mean that he was an opportunist or a Russian agent. Like many other Ukrainian left-wing Socialists, Khvylovy believed in the possibility of political and cultural autonomy for the Ukraine within the framework of the multinational Soviet state. It was thus with the idea of sustaining the Ukrainian cultural revival that, in

2

1920, he began his literary work in Kharkiv. In 1921 he published his first collection of verse, *Molodist* (Youth).

It was, however, his first collection of short stories, *Syni etyudy* (The Blue Etudes, 1923) which brought him fame. All of them were concerned with the revolution in the Ukraine, which Khvylovy greeted with enthusiasm. For him, indeed, this revolution was much more profound and far-reaching than the revolution in Russia. In the Ukraine the revolution aimed at both social justice and national liberation, and in its intensity reached even the extremes of complete anarchism (the rebellion of Makhno). Moreover he regarded the revolution of 1917 in the Ukraine as a continuation of the Cossack risings in the seventeenth century and the peasant rebellions of the eighteenth and nineteenth centuries. In Khvylovy's view what hindered the fullest revolutionary process in the Ukraine was the activity and mentality of the new proletarian philistines. They were the opportunists who regarded the revolution as a mere change of government and hastened to "hang Lenin's picture instead of that of the tsar." Khvylovy's early short stories (a second collection, *Osin* [Autumn] was published in 1924) are full of sketches of these new parasites of the revolution, drawn with all the vehemence and contempt of a romantic revolutionary.

Revolutionary romanticism, which pervades the first story in this collection "Puss in Boots," was thwarted by Khvylovy's gradual disillusionment with communism. Unable to reconcile the dilemma of being a good communist and at the same time a good

3

Ukrainian, Khvylovy portrays in many of his stories the conflict between the communist dream and real life. The tragic proportions of this conflict are best expressed in "Ya" (Myself), a story in which a member of the Cheka, out of a feeling of duty and devotion to the revolution, executed his own mother, an alleged enemy. Having committed this act, the hero realizes his crime and comprehends the depravity and folly of those who believe that "cnds justify means."

In his first novel, *Sanatoriyna zona* (In The Sanatorium District, 1924) Khvylovy worked out the problem of the betrayed revolution in a more subtly symbolic manner. In the sanatorium which represents life in the Soviet state various characters meet, all of whom are victims of the regime. Two men, Khlonya, a former communist idealist, and Anarkh, the ex-leader of a Ukrainian peasant uprising, are now both very sick. Anarkh falls in love with Maya, a beautiful girl who turns out to be a spy of the GPU. In the end both men take their lives while the depressing atmosphere of the sanatorium grows even more forbidding.

Yet another aspect of the same disenchantment in the revolution is treated in the short story "Sentymentalna istoriya" (A Sentimental Tale, 1928). The heroine, an innocent and vigorous peasant girl Bianca, leaves her native village for the town, eager to partake of the radiant "Socialist reality." Very soon, however, surrounded by selfish and lecherous comrades, she becomes utterly disappointed. The only man who offers her any hope of fulfillment is the artist Charhar, who is constantly afraid of denunciations by those who condemn his art on political

4

grounds. Charhar fails to gather enough moral courage to overcome his anxiety and save Bianca by accepting her love; he begins to see in Bianca merely a source of physical pleasure. Yet even in this he fails. Torn between the forces of good and the much more powerful forces of evil, Bianca, to revenge herself on Charhar, gives herself to a disgusting and corrupt official, Kuk. Her innocence lost, she also loses for ever the beautiful dream of a new Soviet society. This story, although almost nauseating in its realism, imparts a sense of the futility at the heart of Soviet life.

By 1925 Khvylovy was the rising star of Soviet Ukrainian literature. "All young writers," commented the literary critic Zerov, "are trying to write like Khvylovy." However, it was not only his literary work which brought him both fame and notoriety in the years that followed. Khvylovy, though a typical angry young man, was very active in literary politics. In the twenties literary life expressed itself mostly in various groups and organizations which generated both the theory and the strategy which these groups followed with or without the approval of the Communist Party.

Still an avowed supporter of the regime, Khvylovy was at first a member of the proletarian literary organization "Hart." After its dissolution late in 1924, he formed, in the following year, a new organization, VAPLITE (Vilna Akademiya Proletarskoyi Literatury—Free Academy of Proletarian Literature) which comprised the elite of the Ukrainian writers of the day (including the poet Tychyna, the novelists Yanovsky, Dosvitny, Panch, Slisarenko, Epik, and the playwright Kulish). In 1925 the Party's attitude to

5

literature was not inflexible. A resolution on literature published in that year by the Central Committee of the Party, was tolerant towards the non-communist, so-called "fellow-traveller" groups, although it prophesied a bright future to the "proletarian" writers, if by their achievements they would prove themselves worthy of hegemony.

In the Ukraine the antagonism between those writers who openly supported the regime and those who were lukewarm towards it was further complicated by the Soviet nationality policy. Yielding to the strong demands by the Ukrainians for cultural freedom, the Communist Party conceded to them virtual autonomy in these matters. It was committed to the policy of the so-called "Ukrainization," which was to establish Ukrainian as the language of administration in that Soviet republic and check the Russification of Ukrainian cities. Taking advantage of this the Ukrainian writers started a big debate on the nature of art and literature and on their place in the Soviet state. In the history of Ukrainian literature this debate is known as the "Literary Discussion." The spark for this controversy, which in the course of three years (1925-28) was fed by over a thousand pamphlets and articles, was provided by Khvylovy.

In an article written in April, 1925, Khvylovy sharply attacked the literary "graphomaniacs, speculators, and other enlighteners" and pleaded that craftsmanship not ideology is the most important prerequisite of literature. "We have not been armed," he wrote, "with the technique a qualified artist must have." The best literary training, he claimed, could be gained by tutelage from the best writers of West-

ern Europe. The West, for Khvylovy, meant even
more than the source of literary excellence; it became
a destination. He explained what he meant with that
characteristic verve which quickens his style but so
often blurs his thought:

> You ask which Europe? Take whichever you
> like: past or present, bourgeois or proletarian,
> the ever-changing one. For indeed: Hamlets,
> Don Juans, or Tartuffes were in the past, but
> they exist also now, they were bourgeois, but
> they are also proletarian; you may think they
> are immortal, but they will be capable of
> change.

> [The ideal man] is the European intellectual
> in the highest sense of this word. He is, if you
> like, the wizard from Wittenberg, so well known
> to us, who revealed to us a magnificent civiliza-
> tion and opened before us boundless perspec-
> tives. He is doctor Faust, if we mean by him the
> questioning spirit of humanity.

The orientation towards Europe which Khvylovy
demanded led him to the logical corollary—"away
from Moscow."

> Since our literature at last can follow its own
> path of development, we are faced with the fol-
> lowing question: "Towards which of the
> world's literatures should it orient itself?"

> On no account towards the Russian. This is
> unconditional. . . . Our poetry must run away

as fast as possible from Russian literature. . . . The point is that Russian literature has been burdening us for ages; it has been the master of the situation, who has trained us to imitate him slavishly.

While the bold watchword of Khvylovy stirred both approval and rebuttal among the litterateurs, the Party grew seriously alarmed. These literary theories propounded by one of its members sounded like dangerous political slogans. It promptly branded Khvylovy as a "bourgeois nationalist." Moreover, Stalin himself considered Khvylovy's ideas obnoxious enough to pass the following condemnation of them in a letter to Kaganovich, made public in 1926:

Khvylovy's demands that the proletariat in the Ukraine be immediately de-Russified, his belief that Ukrainian poetry should keep as far away as possible from Russian literature and style, his pronouncement that "proletarian ideas are familiar to us without the help of Russian art," his passionate belief in some messianic role for the young Ukrainian intelligentsia, his ridiculous and non-Marxian attempt to divorce culture from politics—all this and much more in the mouth of this Ukrainian Communist sounds, and cannot sound otherwise, more than strange. At a time when Western European proletarian classes are full of affection for Moscow . . . this Ukrainian Communist Khvylovy has nothing to say in favor of Moscow except to call on Ukrainian leaders to run away from Moscow as fast as possible. And this is called internationalism . . .

Khvylovy was not, as Stalin charged, divorcing literature from politics. On the contrary, facing the issues squarely, he called for the independent development of Soviet Ukrainian culture which, he believed, would serve the best interest of the Ukrainian SSR and the world revolution. In a pamphlet, *Ukraine or Little Russia*, banned even before publication, he wrote:

> If any one nation shows throughout many centuries a will to express itself as an entity in the form of a state, then all attempts to arrest in one way or another this essential process on the one hand hinder the formation of class forces, and on the other bring an element of chaos into the general historical development of the world. To attempt to rub out independence by empty pseudo-Marxism means a failure to understand that the Ukraine will continue to be an armoury of counter-revolution as long as it does not pass through that essential stage which Western Europe underwent at the time of the formation of national states.

Khvylovy's views were shared by many other Ukrainian writers, artists and scholars. What is even more important, they were well received in some sections of the Ukrainian Communist Party, notably by the Commissar for Education, Oleksander Shumsky. In 1926 the party leaders in Moscow decided to crack

9

down on these "deviations." Both Shumsky and Khvylovy were severely reprimanded. Khvylovy, with some associates from the VAPLITE, wrote a penitent letter to the press and promised to reform. However, his real intention was to continue the opposition to the dictatorial cultural and nationality policy of Moscow. With this aim he helped to edit a magazine *Vaplite,* in which Soviet institutions in the Ukraine and Soviet literary politics were frequently attacked. Only five issues of the journal were allowed to appear, the last of them containing the first installment of Khvylovy's novel *The Woodsnipes* (Valdshnepy). The novel was bitterly attacked by the Party spokesmen as "nationalist," and Khvylovy was forced to destroy the next section of it, to recant in public by writing a letter to the press admitting his "errors," and to see his organization, VAPLITE, dissolved.

Such coercive measures would have subdued anyone but a determined fanatic like Khvylovy. His tactics from then on was to change strategy, to regroup his forces, to form new organizations in place of those dissolved, even to plead guilty, but never to surrender his principles and his fondest hope—that he and his associates would force the Party to abandon the ever-increasing control of Ukrainian culture. A good example of how successful these tactics were may be seen from the journal *Literary Fair* published by Khvylovy's friends in 1929-30. This journal contained some of the sharpest satire of the Soviet regime, veiled in Aesopian language. Khvylovy's satirical stories "Ivan Ivanovich" and "The Inspector General" also belong to this period. In them he emerged as the master of a new style, very different from that of his earlier romantic and impressionistic stories.

Through the untiring efforts of Khvylovy, the opposition to the Party in the Ukraine grew stronger. It embraced not only writers but also the leading theatrical producer Les Kurbas of the famous Kharkiv *Berezil*, Dovzhenko, the film producer with a European fame, prominent artists like Boychuk, Sedlyar, Padalka, Vrona, the economist Volobuyev, and scores of others.

Yet their successes were short lived. In the early 1930's the Party resolved to carry out the First Five-Year Plan and collectivization of agriculture at any cost, and thus a campaign of terror was directed in the Ukraine against the hard core of resistance— Ukrainian culture and literature. In order to subjugate that rebellious nation, the Party resorted not only to the decimation of the population by an artificially created famine, but also to the extermination of the Ukrainian intellectual elite. A special Party emissary, Pavel Postyshev, early in 1933 was invested with despotic powers in the Ukraine. The purge he conducted deprived that country of thousands of its most gifted and devoted citizens. Among its victims was the old Ukrainian Bolshevik, Mykola Skrypnyk, formerly the Commissar of Education, who committed suicide before his arrest in July, 1933. It was in this atmosphere of persecution and terror, when the iron ring around those who had ever opposed or could oppose the regime was closely drawn, that Mykola Khvylovy shot himself on May 13, 1933. His death, which came as a great shock to his friends and followers, marked the end of a courageous fight against communist control of Ukrainian literature.

So much for Khvylovy, the fighter. Yet in following his stormy career, his achievement as a writer must not be forgotten. Because of his political actions the name of "Khvylovism" was given to that brand of "bourgeois--nationalist deviation" which has continued to plague the Soviet state long after his death; but in the field of art his testament was no less impressive.

Much of Khvylovy's work was inspired by the same kind of fervor and enthusiasm for things Ukrainian which was characteristic of the Ukrainian writers of the 19th century. Both had grievances against the powers that ruled their country, both believed in the native genius of the Ukraine. Yet in many other respects Khvylovy parted company with his predecessors. He was sharply opposed to the narrow ethnographical school which idealized peasant life and refused to keep in touch with Western Europe. At the same time he felt that the spirit of Russian literature was alien to the Ukraine. "Russian literature," he wrote, "is above all the literature of pessimism, or rather of passive pessimism . . . In modern Russian ethnographic romanticism we can see the same idealization of Razins and Pugachovs, mixed with a feeling of Russian patriotism and with vague dreams about the future. We cannot go further along that road."

Khvylovy developed his own theory of literature, which he called "romantic vitaism." Its purpose was, as he put it, "to strike yourself and others, to set someone against society, prevent it from falling asleep . . . to reveal the duality of man in our times."

12

It was his aesthetic creed as much as his nationalism which the communists could not accept.

Khvylovy's early short stories (represented in this collection by "Puss in Boots," "Myself," "A Sentimental Tale") were written in a highly impressionist style, full of drama and symbolism. His contrapuntal manner in conjunction with his philosophic and historical interpolations make them difficult to follow in a single reading. Much of his romantic zest for life, especially as it appears in his intensely poetical language and imagery, is inevitably lost in translation. The last two stories in this collection are satires on Soviet officialdom in the Ukraine and on the Ukrainian communists. Their style owes a great deal to the two great satirists, the Ukrainian Gogol and the Irishman Swift, for whom Khvylovy had a great admiration. The five stories contained in this volume are presented in the order in which they were written. They show the transformation of an early communist enthusiast into a cynic, and illustrate a spiritual journey that, in Yeats' words, led to a "desolate heaven."

In the last resort, it is not Khvylovy the disillusioned communist or Khvylovy the nationalist who concerns us here. Here he must be judged on the merit of his works where his true self is best revealed. Under the passion, the drama, and the irony, we may discern the man who wrote of himself: "I passionately love the sky, the grass, the stars, pensive evenings and soft autumn mornings . . . in a word all that perfumes the sadly gay land of our motley life."

GEORGE S. N. LUCKYJ

University of Toronto

PUSS IN BOOTS

There's a colorless word for you: Hapka! Hapka, ay, colorless, and so we called her not Hapka but Comrade Beetle. That's all right—nothing colorless in that. But *haptuvaty*—that's bright, for *haptuvaty* is the same as lacing in gold and silver. . . . There's a laced sunset and a laced sunrise in the shimmer of light at dawn and dusk. *Haptuvaty* is as fragrant as a mead in September or the mown grass in the hay rick—when the scent of the osaka rises in the marshes. Hapka—that's colorless. We called her Comrade Beetle. That does!

Here she is: A real type of a Puss in Boots! Do you know the Puss in Boots in a child's picture book? It is very comic—but warm and close, like the blue-veined hand of an old nanny, like a clear evening amid the gold of autumn. Puss in Boots—that's Comrade Beetle. That's it!

And now I ask you: Where are they from—these Comrade Beetles? How many of them are there? eh? They're come and passed over and through our fragrant red revolution—these Comrade Beetles. "Puss in Boots" passed by.

Ah, I know; that's October's secret. Where they come from, is October's secret.

Today in the steppes I hear no horsemen, nor do I see "Puss in Boots." Vanished to where it came from. Vanished, scattered over the high roads and the suburbs and the country lanes of the republic. "Puss in Boots"—the ants of the Revolution. And today, when the sky is blue-grey and the breeze caresses the brow, my heart is filled with the bluebell's sadness.

Yes! I would sing the song of the wastes of the steppe to these grey ants. Indeed, I would, but—I can't; it should be a song of songs, it should be—an anthem. That's why it is a bluebell's sadness; or shall I compose an anthem for "Puss in Boots" and carry the anthem into the farthest ends of the Republic? Shall I compose an anthem?

This is how she was dressed: A blouse, a skirt (in the winter—an old great-coat), a hat and boots. A khaki blouse without buttons, and khaki—that's green; and the revolution does nothing but bang, rattle, plough and roll over the slopes and wastes, by the pit-heads—wherever the color is khaki. The whole revolution is without buttons, with elbow room, room to stretch oneself, to draw a lung-filling breath in the wide open spaces. Ay, in the wide, wide, world.

A skirt of khaki, too; and if not quite so, near enough, because the color of the wastes had long since stamped itself on it. Yes, a skirt of khaki too. A bit torn in front, a bit behind and a bit at the sides. But no camisole was to be seen, for the revolution knows only one color scheme; red and khaki, so that the camisole was green—shadows of the wastes had fallen on it. There! A cap . . . and on it the pentagonal star. Is that enough for you? Or, under the cap a head shaved—not to suit a fashion—but for the march, for convenience. And to top everything—Boots.

Well, now it's clear: Look at the picture in the child's book. Is it good enough? And now for her looks, and then—for the girl herself.

Looks? Fair? Dark? Why, of course, a beetle. But that's no matter. Eyes . . . oh, those eyes . . . It's not a romance I am writing, but only a little poem. But I must mention her eyes. The Eyes—also a beetle's. Have another look at her eyes; take the ray of an August sun on a blackberry that's what her eyes were like.

And the nose (a disgrace for young ladies) . . . a nose like the head of a tack: snub (Snubby, that was another of her names, only not to her face). And her height? That's obvious: "Puss in Boots." And yet I don't at all want to idealize Comrade Beetle, I only want to write the truth about her—a scrap of truth; for the whole truth—would be a revolution.

Now the reader expects perhaps from me a thrilling story with a thrilling end, and from "Puss in Boots" officially recognized exploits and *beaux gestes*, and so on and so forth. You won't get it. Comrade Beetle and I are none of your bourgeois; there won't be any *beaux gestes* from us. None from Comrade Beetle. If that's what you are after, apply to the lovesick heroes of lovesick poems.

Comrade Beetle—just a "Puss in Boots" with clean gestures and sloe black eyes, going through the wastes of the revolution and, antlike, pulling the weight of the sun and drying the swamps. And what

17

kind?—Oh, you know. Just that!

So you needn't expect a thrilling story or thrilling end from us. For the story starts with—October, and ends with the sunny age we are moving towards.

The end of the story with lovesick poets is . . . "Their lips met—end" or "Oh, my Dulcinea! . . . This dagger I plant in my breast. . . . He dies."

Comrade Beetle and I have nothing to do with that.

True, there are doughty exploits, but not ours. . . . Whose then? Just think!

That's it. This is no novel, only a little song, and I shall soon finish it.

In this chapter I shall relate a little exploit . . . Whose, then? Just think! . . .

Winter, blizzard, snow sweeps, and more snow sweeps . . .

A train, a railway and rails, rails into the steppe.

To the Kuban, the Kuban, the Kuban!

The engine jostles into the goods yard; every time into a goods yard.

The snowy stations stand still and silent; perhaps we shall again retreat, defeated, with bloodshot eyes, and behind the bleak station buildings the wolves will bay at the plaintive cold semaphore. But today we are off to the Kuban, for we trust in our bloodshot eyes.

Comrade Beetle. Yes, there she is, Comrade Beetle. And why she is in this regiment you doubtless don't know and never will know, because I don't know and I don't want to make it up; this is only a scrap of the truth and the whole truth—would be the whole revolution.

At each station nothing but cries of: "The Cossacks! The Cossacks!" Cossacks everywhere, bandits everywhere.

The train pounds on, like the dull oven into the field, like the dull oxen from the field.

The Steppe.

Suddenly: "Stop!"

"What's up?"

"No fuel."

"Comrades! the All-Russian Coal Bunker is in peril!"

Hey, apple, whither rolling with might and main?
You'll get to Krasnov, but never back again.

And suddenly:

Oh, oh, the reapers mowing on the hillside;

"Hey, you Hohols! Why that howling? Enough of this keening—we're gloomy enough without it."

Steppe. Blizzard. Snow sweeps and more snow sweeps.

"Here is Truck No. 5—the international one. Now I'll tell you about the different peoples. There are the Letts—wet and quiet and canny; the Jews—not so bad. The Chinks—Chinese or Tartar—a hard and steadfast folk. And now this Hohol—a keener; when he begins howling about his fields or his girl—hop it!"

The Steppe. Blizzard. And rails . . . rails. "Cossacks!" "Cossacks!"

"Where? What? How?"

"Who is making a panic? You swine!" The six-shooters, pistols and rifles come out in their hundreds. Some look back regretfully, others get out their cartridges while others climb on to the tender and are off; the engine is unhooked and speeds away for fuel.

"Aren't you afraid, Comrade Beetle? The Cossacks."

She laughs; there had been Cossacks in her village. She knows right enough what Cossacks are. And something cast a gloom over her, she became lost in thought.

. . . For a long time nothing but the wide fields. It is a long time till the engine is back. It is back at last. And again it's off into the wild and silent steppe. . . . From station to station, from cold night to cold night. No fuel. At night the station fences crack and crack and the tattered trucks, all in holes, gape sadly.

"The Train of General X."

From the lone station to cold night, from lone night to cold station.

Comrade Beetle has found fuel. Like this:

"Give me just this log, old lady!"

"What?"

"Just this log."

"Take it then."

She took it.

"Perhaps another one, eh?"

The Old Lady looks at her: Beetle: Puss in Boots.

She gives her some more.

Comrade Beetle laughs: "Ha, ha! Done the old lady."

She hadn't done her at all, she is just—the Beetle!

Oh, these beetles in boots, really they give me no peace! When I am a famous writer I'll write a great drama in verse: "Puss in Boots."

The crackling of an iron stove—fuel. The wild blizzard races and rages after the truck. We are off to the Kuban. . . . Up . . . (That's Comrade Beetle.) Up . . . down . . . The truck's complement is round the stove; perhaps it's someone else or perhaps it's us—all of us. She teaches us how to mend a burn in a great coat.

But she says: "Stop that fooling. Do you think that when you are home I shall knock around with you as I am doing now? Shoo! Not by a long chalk! . . . Here you are, sew!"

She makes our dinner for us—she is our cook—That's all.

She is non-party, but she has a fat book in her knapsack—"The Meaning of Communism" (Anonymous) . . . Edition of the X Sector of the Workers' and Peasants' Red Army.

And again we say to her: "I say, Comrade Beetle! What about having a beano with you?" And her answer was "Shoo!"

We guffaw, for we know that Shoo isn't said to them all—we have a young laddy—that's what we call him, laddy. He's snub-nosed too, and we've noticed him putting his arms round her, and she's mum. . . . Well, that's their affair.

But she astounded us after all; sometimes she'd use words and make remarks that would set us gaping. When we were thinking only about the enemy she would have something else in her head.

"Did you get into the sixth form at school?" Someone would say with a laugh.

She clapped her hands in amusement.

"The sixth and forms? They are for the gentry."

For us it was—"shoo!"

Then an uncouth hohol said in a tone of authority: "That's the regimental Lenin . . ."

"Yes, chapped hands."

. . . And their longing lurked behind the window pane, longing dropped from the wire, which ran along and followed the telegraph posts into the unknown. . . . Blizzard, frost, stations with snow-covered bells, occasionally longing on the wire, and all the time: "Hah! Revolution—is revolution!"

And then again the cold trucks, the long trains, trains like oxen, and suddenly:

"Stop!"

"What's up?"

"No fuel."

The engine is unhitched, the engine speeds into the dark wild blizzard, into the wild silent steppe.

But I have forgotten to say: Often when the train stopped at a station "for an indeterminate period" Comrade Beetle, her work at the field kitchen over, would go away from the truck God knows where, and be away for a long time. And she would always come back pensively. Why pensively. That will appear further on.

Posters, Posters, Posters . . . Hu! Hu! Bang! Bang! Posters! Posters! Posters! East, West, North, South. Russia, Ukraine, Siberia, Poland. Turkestan, Georgia, White Russia, Azerbaidjan, Crimea, Khiva, Bokhara.

Posters! Posters! Posters! Germans, Poles, Petlyura —etc., etc., etc. . . . Kolchak, Yudenich, Denikin— etc., etc., etc. . . .

Posters! Posters! Posters! One month, two three, six, twenty . . . etc., etc., etc. . . . Hu! Hu! Bang! Bang!

The months speed past. Passed . . . I don't know how many passed; perhaps it was yesterday, perhaps the day before, or perhaps 200 years ago? When was it? . . . Perhaps it is a—bluebell dream. I don't know!

And now again—summer, the summer of the steppes. They are the steppes by the Dnieper—not far away is the Dnieper. . . . Now the nights in the summer steppes. It is so wonderful, so moving!

You know? You sit in the steppe and think of feather grass. It is so wonderful; thinking of the feather grass, when it rustles mysteriously, like the hey presto of a rabbit's scut. It is so wonderful! Oh, how sorry I am that my predecessors have described the steppe at night before me. Or else I would have described it. Yes, indeed!

. . . I arrived. I received a note on the third day. "Comrade, you came, I think, on Friday. You are requested to register immediately at the cell."

I said: "The secretary, tough proposition, likely enough an old party member."

The comrade laughed: "The note surprises you? . . . That's a trifle. Now, you'll have to have a taste of the discussion. I am fed up with these discussions."

My interest awoke. "What discussions?"

"Wait a bit, you'll see for yourself." And he didn't

23

tell me.

I went off. "Where is the room of the Communist cell?"

"There!"

I enter.

I look—rather familiar, I think. I make a guess and suddenly I remember; the self same Puss in Boots.

That's got it!

"You the Secretary of the Communist cell?"

"I am" . . .

"You, if I am not wrong, are Comrade Beetle?"

"Yes."

"We know each other then. You remember?"

She, of course, remembers everything; but first she entered my party ticket and only then did she speak. "Of course: it is So and So, long ago." Comrade Beetle had since read "The Meaning of Communism" (Anonymous) Edition of the X Sector of the Workers' and Peasants' Red Army. And that's all. Apart from that it is so simple: Puss in Boots talks over the wastes of the revolution and perhaps does not even know that she is the Secretary of the Communist cell, and only then finds it out and writes down: "You are requested to register without delay" . . . But I wasn't really astonished, you know; especially as so long a time had passed, and even then Puss in Boots was—"the regimental Lenin" . . . And, to be candid, the second edition of Lenin: "regimental Lenin"—also was sometimes stark and harsh.

That's the picture. I was at fault.

Comrade Beetle's eyes flashed like a dragon. "Comrade! Aren't you ashamed?"

"Allow me . . . I really . . . I . . ."

Comrade Beetle's eyes flashed like a dragon: "Your party ticket! . . . Hand it over!"

I hand it over.

She writes down: "Comrade So and So in such and such a month failed to attend so many meetings. He has been officially reprimanded by the Secretary of the Communist cell and warned that his lack of discipline will be brought before the public opinion of the party at the party tribunal with a view of his degradation to the stage of candidate or his definitive exclusion from our communist ranks." Signature. Full stop. Concise! Clear!

I: "just a bit. Well . . . nothing."

Of course, as then (then in the wild steppe) she has her khaki on, for the revolution knows only one color scheme; red with khaki. As then, gigantic misfitting boots. As then; "Shoo!"

As then, the eyes like sloes laugh and nose like sloes —head of a tack, snub.

As then there were nights, but not cold now, warm, shimmering—the summer nights of the steppe. But now it was not the Cossacks harrying us, but bandits from the woods harrying our rear. From the South we are pressed on by an enraged, wounded bear at bay from the white lair of the Great Russian Empire.

And now that discussion (we are fed up with it). There is a phrase—hold yourself in check and don't forget the Cheka. We paraphrased it into: Discussion —hold yourself in check so as not to fall into the secretarial Cheka.

Comrade Beetle says: "The discussion to-night!"

We: "Oh! Oh! We are fed up!" (This of course not aloud.)

"Comrade, give me a look at 'The ABC of Communism'."

"Oh, don't worry me, comrade. Now, I've forgotten; how does it go? Damn! Come along. Capitalism has three characteristics: Hired labor . . . hired labor . . . hired labor . . ."

Someone prompts him: "The monopolization of the means of production. And . . ."

"Go to the devil! I know it fine myself."

And then at the other end: "I say! How flushed you've all got!"

"Comrade Larikov, now aren't you flushed?"

"I don't think. Don't tell me you know everything." (This to one of the know-alls.)

"Well, if you know everything, tell me this: When did Thiers destroy the great French Commune—in '71 or in '48? Eh? Out with it."

"And you, Comrade Molodchikov, don't fox, don't try to get out of it, say frankly that you don't know. Then I'll tell you." Molodchikov blushes, I blush and lots of us blush, for most of us are ignoramuses, but we wouldn't ever own up.

"What bosh—these discussions, as if we were school kids!"

"That's right. The very devil! It's a bourgeois way of education. We might just as well have an exam with inspectors!"

A voice again: "Won't you give me the ABC of Communism for an instant?"

"Oh, damn it! I've forgotten it again. Capitalism has three characteristics: The monopolization of production . . . the monopolization of production . . ."

"You see, you don't know it a bit."

26

"Oh, clear off, comrade."

At last the evening. Yes; outside, as in other stories of mine (not all)—thundering guns, and somewhere in the tall grass, and then on the road—cavalry. Ours? We are told it's not ours. Whose then? I don't know. Perhaps the enemy's. Perhaps a raid.

And someone, in a whisper, following from the high grass—"Perhaps to-morrow, here, where we are sitting, there'll be waste paper, litter and the smell of desertion, the smell of desertion, the smell of retreat, the smell of blood."

But these things are forgotten.

The reader finished his report.

Comrade Beetle: "Well, Comrade Boyko, I haven't understood anything all the same. What's all this about dialectics, if the subject is historical materialism? How can you explain that?"

"Excuse me, Comrade Chairman, as a matter of fact, I wasn't going to speak."

Comrade Beetle's eyes flashed like a dragon: "As chairman I have nothing to excuse, but as a comrade I request you to speak."

We spoke, we got mixed (some of us even got rather sick). And all this was called the discussion.

Comrade Beetle said: "Shoo! Wrong! And now you, Comrade Molodchikov?"

She was definitely dropping into the part of a teacher. And we were getting furious, as we had our own pride. We were enraged with our ex-cook, with today's secretary of the Communist Cell, with Puss in Boots.

Then she would run round, fuss, assemble the women, organize the women's gatherings, where the subjects were: Abortion, love, the rights of a cook (Lenin said).

Cries of: "Down with the family! Long live the woman bachelor!"

And about the child-bearing woman they were saying: "There must be state lying-in homes, there must be communal laundries, and so on and so forth."

"Comrade, may you love two at the same time?"

"That depends on your understanding of historical materialism." My knowledge of it is rotten, so I stand down.

———

Well then—

I could write a lot more about Comrade Beetle, a very interesting business. But you see it's just half-past four, and I must hurry up for the party meeting, for there—Comrade Beetle No. 2 and that means . . . but, if you are Party, you know yourself what that means.

———

This is what she wrote: "Comrade Mykola (that's me, Mykola Khvylovy). You, if I am right, will, by the day after tomorrow, be in the Tarashcha regiment, and I in the reserve cavalry; there is some Makhno business there—we must agitate. Perhaps we shall never see each other again, so I want to ask you not to be angry about the discussion. I know that you have your pride, but the whole lot of us are ignorant. And, in so far as the dictatorship is ours. . . . In short, you understand me; we must grow up in a year or two not an inch, but a whole yard. With Communist greetings. Beetle."

But she didn't go that day, and we did meet again.

This is where we met. Picture an empty school, political department. Comrades sleeping in the corners and on the tables. The ants of the revolution. Some of them go to the regiments, the inspection, others will stay on here, and afterwards will also go—to the regiments, the inspection. This is the training school of the revolution.

It was bright, and then it got dark—the clouds were passing. A drizzling rainstorm came pouring down. It rained, it rained, and for some reason I felt sad. I wanted to drop off as soon as I could. But there was a deal of sniffling going on in the corner stopping me from sleeping.

"Comrade, don't keep me from sleeping."

Silence. The rainstorm beat gently and monotonously against the window. I longed for it and the rattling carts to stop; they reminded me of the hard road to Moscow—going away to Moscow, northwards away from the enemy's raids.

"Comrade, don't keep me from sleeping."

Silence.

Perhaps you have guessed already that it was Comrade Beetle who was sniffling.

She came up to me: "Let us be off!" I looked at her in amazement.

We went out into the porch. Nothing but the grey road into the night steppe and the rain.

"Were you crying?"

"I was!" And she laughed: "Just a bit ashamed . . . you know . . . it gets you like that."

And she told me all about it.

And so I learned that even Comrade Beetle, beetle and puss in boots though she is, could feel sad, and it

29

wasn't always "Shoo!" with her.

Then the little snub nose told me that she wasn'
19, as we thought, but really 25, and that she had had
a bastard, just a little bastard—a Cossack had hanged
it on a lamp-post. That was in the Far East, but she
still felt it. That was in her Far East, when she wen
away with the commando. And that was the Cossack'
revenge.

I remembered the snowy steppe. The rain came
down. The same grey road and the dark shadows o
the buildings.

———

But there wasn't anything in it after all, that the
had hanged the kid on a lamp-post; there's been
worse than that. I don't mean to draw the tears from
you.

And here's a little exploit—no doubt of that. And
whose? Just think! Comrade Beetle No. 2 . . . No.
. . . No. 4 . . . and I don't know how many more.

There is no Comrade Beetle No. 1. "Puss in
Boots" has vanished into the hidden entrails of th
republic. Comrade Beetle has vanished.

Puss in Boots is stalking over the wastes of th
revolution, pulling the weight of the sun and dryin
the swamp, which one—you know. So; the pries
christened her Hapka, a colorless word, and from
haptuvaty—lacing in gold and silver—everything
bright. We called her—Comrade Beetle. And histor
will call her—Puss in Boots.

Puss in Boots—a type. Full stop. Concise! Clear
that's all.

———

Translated by N. B. Jopson and D. S. Mirsky.

MY SELF
(ROMANTICA)

From distant misty regions, from the calm lakes of the intangible Commune[1] there rustles a whisper: Maria is coming. I go out into the boundless fields, pass over the hilly crests, walk in the place where the tumuli glow, and lean against a solitary desert rock. I look into the distance. Thought after thought, galloping like Amazons, swarms around me. Then everything disappears. The mysterious Amazons, swaying rhythmically, fly towards the horned tips of the mountains, and the day darkens. The road speeds on amid the hillocks, and after it—the silent steppe. I raise my eyelids and try to recollect . . . in truth, my mother—the prototype incarnate of that extraordinary Maria who stands on the boundaries of ages unknown. My mother — simplicity, silent grief, and boundless kindness. (This I well remember). And both my intolerable suffering and my unbearable torture grow warm in the lamp of fanaticism before this wonderful picture of sorrow.

---

[1] Khvylovy often uses the image of the "Intangible Commune," "Distant Commune," or "Commune beyond the hills," to convey his dream of an ideal communist state.

Mother says that I (her rebellious son) have absolutely tortured myself to death. Then I take her lovely head, sprinkled with silvery grey, and rest it on my bosom. Behind the window dewy mornings pass and pearl-drops fall. Intolerable days move on. In the distance, out of the dark forest, wayfarers trudge, stopping by the blue fountain, where the roads flow in all directions, where stands the highway cross. They are young people from beyond the mountains.

But the nights pass, evenings rustle near the poplars, the poplars withdraw into the unknown distance of the path, and following them—ages, years and my turbulent youth. These are the days before the thunderstorm. There, beyond the montainous slope of the blue fir forest the lightnings flash and thicken, and the mountains foam. A heavy suffocating thunder can scarcely tear itself out of India, out of the Orient. And Nature grows weary on the eve of the storm. And yet, beyond the cloudy fog may be heard yet another roar—a dull cannonade. Onward move the two storms.

"Terror!" Mother says that she has watered the mint today, and that the mint is wilting with sorrow. Mother says: "A storm is coming up!" And I see in her eyes two crystal dews.

I

Attack follows attack. The enemy's regiments press on furiously. Then our cavalry flanks and the phalanxes of the insurgents move in a counterattack, while the storm grows, and my thoughts tauten unbearably, like wire.

Night and day I am disappearing into the *Cheka*.[2]

Our living quarters are in a fantastic palace; it is the mansion of an executed noble, with gorgeous door-curtains, ancient pictures, portraits of the princely family. All these gaze at me from every corner of my improvised office.

Somewhere the military telephone drawls out its sorrowful, terrifying threnody like a distant station siren.

On a luxurious sofa sits an armed Tartar, legs crossed beneath him, monotonously chanting the Asiatic: "Ala-la-la."

I look at the portraits: the prince is knitting his brows, the princess exhibits a haughty contempt, the princelings play in the gloom of century-old oaks. Among this extraordinary austerity I feel the entire ancient world, the whole impotent grandeur of it, and the beauty of the past years of nobility. It is obviously like setting mother-of-pearl at a banquet in a wild and famished land. And I, a complete stranger, a bandit, according to one terminology, an insurgent, according to another, I look frankly and unflinchingly at these portraits, and there is no longer any anger in my soul, nor will there ever be any.

And I realize that I am a *chekist*,[3] but still I remain a human being. On a murky night, behind the window, when the urban evenings pass (the palace had flown up and lords it over the city), when small columns of blue smoke rise above the brick factory,

---

[2] *Cheka*—the Extraordinary Commission for Protection against Counter-revolution (secret police).

[3] *Chekist*, a member of the *Cheka*.

and the citizens creep like mice, my comrades pass
through the gates and into the canary castle, and
meet on a murky night in my unusual office. This is
a new Sanhedrin, this is the dark tribunal of the
Commune.

Then from every corner leers death, the real and
truly terrible.

A citizen: "Here sadism presides!"

I: . . . (I am silent).

On the city tower beyond the mountain pass, a
metallic sound rings out alarmingly. It is the clock
striking. From the darkling steppe a dull cannonade
is heard.

My comrades are sitting around a large table made
of dark wood. Silence. (Only the distant horn of the
telephone again drawls out its sorrowful, terrifying
melody). Behind the window, from time to time, pass
the insurgents.

It is easy to recognize my comrades: Doctor Tahabat, Andrusha, the third—a degenerate (a faithful
sentinel stationed on guard). The dark tribunal is
in full session.

I: "Attention! The first item to be considered is
the case of the merchant X!"

From distant chambers the footmen appear, bowing as they did before the princes; they look search-
ingly at the new Sanhedrin and place tea on the table
Then they vanish, moving inaudibly on velvety car-
pets, in the labyrinths of lofty rooms.

The candelabrum burns dimly. It is difficult for
the light to illumine even a quarter of the office. Up
above, the chandelier can hardly be discerned. The

city is dark. And here it is dark; the electric power-plant has been put out of order.

Doctor Tahabat sprawls at ease on the large sofa further away from the candelabrum, and I can see only his receding white forehead. Behind him, still further in obscurity, stands the faithful sentry with the degenerate skull structure. I can only see his rather foolish eyes, but I know he has a low forehead, a crop of black dishevelled hair, and a flat nose. He always reminds me of a convict, and I think his name must have figured more than once in criminal reports.

Andrusha sits near me with a distracted look and from time to time glances anxiously at the doctor. I know why. Andrusha, my poor Andrusha, has been assigned to the *Cheka* by the revolutionary committee against his feeble will. And whenever Andrusha, this unhappy communard,[4] has to place a forceful signature under the somber decision "to be executed," he always hesitates, always signs thus: not a name, not a surname on the austere, vital documents, but a completely incomprehensible, absolutely fantastic tail, like a Chinese hieroglyph.

I: "The case is complete. Doctor Tahabat, what do you think?"

The doctor (dynamically): "To be executed!"

Andrusha looks at Tahabat somewhat alarmed,

---

[4] Literally, a member or supporter of the Paris commune of 1871. Frequently used by Khvylovy instead of "communist" in order to remove the story from contemporary life and to emphasize the ideal character of revolution.

and hesitates. Finally, in a tremulous, irresolute voice he says: "I don't agree with you, doctor."

"You don't agree with me?"—and a rumble of hoarse laughter rolls into the dim chambers of the princes.

I am expecting this laughter. It is always so. But this time I shudder, and seem to be sinking into a cold marsh. My swift thought approaches its culmination. And at that very moment the picture of my mother suddenly rises before me. "To be executed?" And my mother looks at me calmly, sorrowfully.

Again on the distant city tower beyond the mountain pass the metallic sound rings out: it is the clock striking. Darkness from the north. The dull cannonade can hardly be heard in this dwelling of princes. A message is telephoned: our men have started a counter-attack. Behind the tapestry, through the glass-door, glares the redness of the sky: beyond the distant mounds villages are burning, steppes are burning, and the city dogs howl at the conflagration. The city is silent, and hearts ring out to each other in the silence.

Doctor Tahabat presses a button. A footman brings old wines on a tray. He withdraws, and his steps melt on the leopard skins.

I look at the candelabrum, but my glance, in spite of myself, steals to where Doctor Tahabat and the sentinel are sitting. In their hands they hold bottles of wine, and they drink passionately, savagely. I think, "It has to be so." But Andrusha moves restlessly from place to place, continually trying to say something. I know what he is thinking: he wants to say that it is not decent, that the communards are not used to such things, that this is—a bacchanal, etc., etc.

Ah, how strange is this communard Andrusha!

But when Doctor Tahabat throws the empty bottle on the velvet carpet and very carefully signs his name under the decision—"To be executed," despair suddenly seizes me. This doctor, high of forehead and white in his baldness, with his cold reasoning, and a stone instead of a heart—is he not both my irresistible master and my beastly instinct? Head of the black tribunal of the Commune though I am, in his hands I am merely an insignificant thing which has surrendered to a savage will.

"But is there a way out?"

"A way out?"—But I see no way out.

Then there rushes past me the dark history of civilization, with its peoples, ages, and Time itself.

But I see no way out!

Indeed, truth stands behind Doctor Tahabat.

Andrusha hurriedly scribbles under the decision, while the degenerate, smacking his lips, stares at the letters. I think: "If the doctor is an evil genius, my evil will, then the degenerate is an executioner." But again I think: "Ah, what nonsense! For is he an executioner? Was it not to him, to this sentinel of the black tribunal that I composed hymns in moments of great tension?"

And then my mother—the prototype of the ideal Maria—withdraws from me and waits, rigid, in the darkness.

The candles are melting. The austere shapes of the prince and the princess dissolve into the blue mist of cigarette smoke.

The execution is decreed.

Six!

Enough! Enough for tonight!

The Tartar again drawls out his Asiatic "ala-la-la." I gaze at the door curtain and at the conflagration of the sky through the glass of the door. Andrusha has already disappeared. Tahabat and the sentinel are drinking old wines. I throw a gun over my shoulder and leave the dwelling of princes. I walk down the silent, deserted streets of the besieged city.

The city is dead. The citizens know that in three or four days we shall have disappeared, that our counter-attacks are in vain. Soon our wagons will rumble towards the cold, distant regions. The city skulks. Obscurity.

In dark, burly silhouette in the east stands the palace of the princes, now the dark tribunal of the Commune. I turn and look at it, and suddenly recall that there are six lives on my conscience.

Six on my conscience?

No, it is not true. Six hundred, six thousand, six million—numberless hosts are on my conscience!

Numberless hosts?

And I press my head with my hands.

And again there rushes past me the somber history of civilization, the peoples, the ages, and Time itself.

Exhausted, I lean on a fence, go down on my knees, and passionately bless my first meeting with Doctor Tahabat and the sentinel with the degenerative structure of the skull. Then I turn and gaze pleadingly at that gloomy eastern silhouette.

I lose myself in the alleys. Finally, I come to the solitary cottage where my mother lives. The yard smells of mint. Behind the shed the lightning flashes, and the rumble of stifled thunder is heard.

Darkness!

I enter the room, take off my gun and light a candle. "Are you asleep?" But Mother is not asleep. She approaches, takes my weary face in her dry old palms, and rests her head on my breast. Once more she says that I, her rebellious son, have absolutely tortured myself to death. And on my hands I feel the crystal dews, falling from her eyes.

I: "Ah, mother how tired I am!"

She draws me towards the candlelight and looks at my weary face. Then she stops to look sorrowfully at the icon of Maria. I know! My mother is ready to enter a nunnery tomorrow: She cannot stand our horrors, and everything she sees is savage to her.

But on the point of reaching the bed I shudder: "Savage? How dare my mother think that? Only the Versaillais[5] think that!"

And then, perplexed, I assure myself that it is not true, that there is no mother before me, only a phantom. "A phantom?" and I shudder again.

No, that is not true! Here, in this quiet room, my mother is not a phantom but a part of my criminal "self" to which I impart my will. Here, in this dull cranny, on the outskirts of the city, I am hiding one part of my soul from the guillotine.

Then in a beastly ecstasy I close my eyes, and like an animal in early Spring, babble and whisper: "Who wants to know the details of my experiences?

––––
[5] Versaillais—supporter of the King during the French Revolution; here, defenders of the old order.

I am a real communard. Who dares gainsay me? Have I not the right to a moment's rest?"

Feebly the lamp burns before the icon of Maria. And in front of the lamp, like a statue, stands my sorrowful mother. But I no longer think of anything. A tender, quiet sleep strokes my head.

II

Our men are withdrawing from position to position: there is panic at the front, there is panic at the rear. My battalion is ready. In two days, I, too, shall throw myself into the cannon's roar. My battalion is composed of young fanatics of the Commune.

But just now I am no less necessary here. I know what the rear means when the enemy is at the city walls. Vague rumors increase daily, creeping like snakes down the streets. They even begin to disquiet the garrisoned companies.

It is reported to me: "Subdued complaints are heard." "A revolt is likely to break out." Yes! Yes! I know a revolt is likely to break out, and my faithful agents scour the alleys, and already there are not enough prisons for this guilty, yet almost innocent city rabble.

The cannonade draws nearer and nearer. Messengers from the front are more frequent. Dust gathers in clouds and hangs above the city, concealing the misty, fiery sun. From time to time there are flashes of lightning. The wagon-trains move in a line, engines clamor alarmingly, the cavalry men dash past.

But at the somber tribunal of the Commune broods an oppressive quiet.

Yes: there will be hundreds of executions, and it staggers me!

Yes: the Versaillais already hear the clear short shots tearing the dead, reverberating silence of the estate of the princes above the city. The Versaillais now: Dukhonin's staff!

While the mornings blossom with mother of pearl, and the early stars fall into the mist of the distant pine forest. . . .

While the dull cannonade increases . . .

Thunder threatens increasingly: soon there will be a storm.

. . . .

I enter the palace of the princes. Doctor Tahabat and the sentinel are drinking wine. Andrusha is sitting in a corner, downcast. Then Andrusha comes up to me and naively and sorrowfully says: "Listen, friend! Let me go!"

I: "Where to?"

Andrusha: "To the front. I cannot remain here any longer."

Aha! He cannot remain here any longer! And all of a sudden anger flares up within me. Finally it breaks out. I have been restraining myself for a long time. He wants to go to the front? He wants to be far away from this dirty filthy work? He wants to wipe his hands of it and become as innocent as a dove? He transfers to me his right to bathe in puddles of blood?

Then I cry out: "You forget yourself! Do you hear? If you mention this again I will have you executed at once."

41

Doctor Tahabat, energetically: "Yes, him! Yes, him!" and his laughter rolls down the deserted labyrinths of the palace of the princes—"Yes, him! Yes, him!"

Andrusha withers, grows pale and leaves the office.

The doctor says: "Period! I will take a rest! You continue to work!"

I: "Who is next?"

"Case no. 282."

I: "Bring them in."

The sentinel goes out of the room silently, like an automaton. (Yes, he is an irreplaceable sentinel: not Andrusha alone—we too have sinned: the doctor and I. We often neglected to witness the executions. But he, this degenerate, was always a soldier of the revolution, and would leave the field of execution only when the gun-smoke had melted away and the corpses were being buried.)

The tapestry parts and two persons come into my office: a woman in mourning and a man with a pince-nez. They are frightened by the setting: aristocratic luxury, the portraits of the princes, and disorder—empty bottles, revolvers, and the blue cigarette smoke.

I: "Your family?"

"Z!"

"Your family?"

"Y!"

The man contracts his pale lips and falls into an unpardonably whimpering tone: he begs for mercy. The woman is wiping her eyes with a piece of cloth.

I: "Where were you taken from?"

"From such and such a place!"

"Why were you taken?"

"For so and so!"

Ah, there was a meeting at your place! How could meetings be held in such alarming times, at night, and in a private residence!

Ah, you are theosophists! You are seeking Truth! New Truth? Yes! Who is it? Christ? No? Another saviour of the world? Yes! Yes! You are not content with Confucius, nor with Buddha, nor with Mahomet, nor with the devil himself! Ah, I understand: it is necessary to fill the empty place.

I: "Then according to you, the time has arrived for the coming of a new Messiah?"

The man and woman: "Yes!"

I: "Do you think that this psychological crisis is to be observed in Europe and in Asia, and in every part of the world?"

The man and woman: "Yes!"

I: "Then why in the devil's name don't you make the Cheka into this Messiah?"

The woman bursts into tears. The man grows paler. The austere portraits of the prince and princess look down gloomily from the walls. From a distance come the terrifying sounds of the station, and the cannonade is heard. The enemy's armored train presses down upon our positions—it is reported by telephone. A great din rises out of the city: the military wagons rumble on the pavement.

The man falls to his knees and begs for mercy. I push him away forcefully with my foot—and he falls backwards. The woman presses her mourning veil to her temple and bends over the table in despair. The woman says dully and tonelessly: "Listen, I am the mother of three children!"

I: "To be executed!"

The sentinel springs forward at once, and in half a minute there is no one in the office. Then I go up to the table, pour some wine from the decanter, and drink it in a draught. Then I place my hand on my cold forehead and say: "Next!"

The degenerate comes in. He advises me to postpone the following cases and to consider a case which is not on the list: a new group of the Versaillais had just been brought in from the city, all nuns it seems; in the city hall square they have openly agitated against the Commune.

I am entering into my role. A mist forms before my eyes, and I am in a state which may be described as an extraordinary ecstasy. I imagine that in such a state the fanatics went to the Holy Wars. I walk up to the window and say: "Bring them in!"

A whole crowd of nuns packs into my office. I feel rather than see this; I am looking at the city. Evening is drawing on—I do not turn for quite a while; I am enjoying the thought that in two hours they will all be no more! Evening is drawing on. And again the storm-heralding lightning is rending the landscape.

On the distant horizon, behind the brick-factory. smoke rises. The Versaillais are pressing on wrathfully and ardently—it is reported by telephone. From time to time the wagon-trains emerge upon the deserted tracts and hurriedly withdraw northwards. The cavalry sentinel detachments stand out in the steppe like the distant valiant knights of old.

Alarm.

In the city the shops are closed. The city is dead and moves away into a wild, medieval distance. Up in the sky, stars are sprouting and rain down on the earth a sickly green light. Then they pale and vanish.

But I must hurry! Behind my back there is a group of nuns! Yes, I must hurry! The cellar is filled to capacity.

I turn resolutely and want to say the irrevocable: "To be executed."

. . . .

But I turn and see—straight in front of me, my mother, my sorrowing mother with the eyes of Maria.

I dart to one side in anxiety: what is it—hallucination? I dart to the other side in alarm and cry out: "You?"

And from the crowd of women I hear the sorrowful: "Son! My rebellious son!"

I feel as though I am at the point of collapse. I am dazed, I grasp a chair and lean over it. But at that very moment a rumbling laugh rolls, strikes against the ceiling and is lost. It is Doctor Tahabat: "Mother? Ah, you, devil's pup! Suckling! 'Mother'?" I become myself in a trice and grasp my gun. "Hell!" and I throw myself upon the doctor.

But he looks at me coldly and says: "Well, well, not so loud, you, traitor to the Commune! See that you arrange matters with 'mother' (he emphasizes 'mother'), even as you have with others." He withdraws in silence.

I am silent. I stand pale, almost lifeless before the silent group of nuns, my eyes wandering, and like a wolf at bay. (I can see this in the gigantic mirror which is hanging opposite me.)

45

Yes! At last they have seized the other end of my soul! No longer will I go to the outskirts of the city to hide myself, as a criminal. Now I have but one right: never to mention to anyone that my heart is broken in two.

I do not lose my head. Thoughts are slashing at my brain. What must I do? Will I, a soldier of the revolution, shrink from my duty at this moment of decision? Shall I leave my post and betray the Commune so shamelessly?

Pressing my jaws tightly, I look at my mother with a frown, and say sharply: "Take them all to the cellar. I will be there shortly." But I have hardly finished saying this when my office again shakes with laughter. Then I turn to the doctor and say emphatically: "Doctor Tahabat: You apparently forget with whom you are dealing! Do you, too, want to join Dukhonin's staff—with this rabble?" and I motion to where my mother stands, and I leave the office in silence.

Behind me I hear nothing.

From the palace I go, like one intoxicated, nowhere in particular, into the dusk of the stifling hot, storm-threatening evening. The cannonade is increasing. Above the distant brick-factory smoke rises. Beyond these confines rumble the armored cars, continuing a stubborn duel. The enemy's regiments press ardently upon the insurgents. There is a smell of executions.

I am going nowhere in particular. Past me move the wagon-trains; cavalry-men dash by, and tanks rumble down the pavement. The city is covered with dust, and the evening does not relieve the atmosphere of the threatening storm.

I am going nowhere in particular. Without a thought, with a dull vacancy, a heavy load on my stooped shoulders.

I am going nowhere in particular.

Yes, these are intolerable moments. It is torture. But I already know what I shall do.

I knew it even when I left the palace. Otherwise I would not have left the office so quickly.

But I must be consistent. And throughout the evening I ponder these matters. During the few dark hours, short clear shots flash periodically.

I, the head of the somber tribunal of the Commune, am performing my duties with respect to the Revolution. And is it my fault that the picture of my mother does not leave me for a moment during that night? Is it my fault?

At noon Andrusha comes and mutters somberly: "Listen, let her go!"

I: "Who?"

"Your mother!"

I: (I am silent).

Then, painfully, I feel like laughing. I cannot restrain myself and laugh out loud into all the chambers. Andrusha looks at me sternly. He is not at all what he used to be. "Listen, why this melodrama?" This time my naive Andrusha wants to be clever. But he is mistaken.

I: (roughly) "Be off!"

But even this time Andrusha does not pale.

Ah, this naive communard, apparently, does not

understand anything. He literally does not know why this senseless, beastly cruelty should be. He sees nothing behind my cold wooden features.

I: "Telephone! Find out where the enemy is!"

Andrusha: "Listen!"

I: "Telephone! Find out where the enemy is!"

At this moment a shell seethes above the palace and explodes nearby. The windows jingle, and the echo reverberates down the loud, empty chambers.

The telephone reports that the Versaillais are pressing and are already close: about three versts away. Cossack scouts have been seen near the station: the insurgents are withdrawing. The distant siren at the railway station is wailing.

Andrusha leaps out. I follow him.

Smoke covers everything. On the horizon fires are seen flashing again. Above the city the dust hovers in clouds. The sun is like copper, and the sky is hidden. Only a mountainous, turbid cloud of dust moves hastily across the distant arc of heaven. Fantastic eddies are roused up from the road, dash upwards, fly over the settlements, on and on. It is as if the threatening storm were enchanted.

Nearby, the cannon are thundering. The cavalrymen are dashing about. Tanks and wagon-trains are withdrawing northward.

I forget everything. I hear nothing—and do not even remember how I come to find myself in the cellar.

Shrapnel spatters near me, and the yard outside clears rapidly. I approach the door, wanting only to peep through a small window to see where my mother is sitting, when somebody takes me by the hand. I turn—the degenerate. "What a guard! They have all fled! Ha! Ha!"

I: "You?"

He: "Is it me? Of course it's me!" and he knocks at the door with his finger.

Yes, he is a faithful dog of the revolution. He would stand on guard even under the fiercest fire! I remember thinking "He is the sentinel of my soul," as I trudge toward the city wilderness without a thought in my head.

Towards evening the southern district is taken. We are forced to move north, leaving the city. But the insurgents are commanded to remain until nightfall, and steadfastly they die on the ramparts, in the trenches, at the crossroads, and in the silent corners of the city.

But what about me?

A hurried evacuation is in progress, and clear, sharp firing is going on on both sides.

In the end, I am on the point of collapse!

Documents are being burnt. Hostage parties are being sent away. The remainder of the requisitions are being collected.

In the end, I am on the point of collapse!

But my mother's face would suddenly appear, and I would hear again her sorrowful and persistent voice.

I throw my hair back and with widened eyes look at the city tower. Once again evening draws on, and again the settlements in the south are ablaze.

The somber tribunal of the Commune prepares for flight. The transportation wagons are being loaded, the wagon-trains plod onward, and throngs of people hasten north. Only a solitary armored train dies away in the depths of the pine forest, and checks the advance of the enemy's regiments on the right flank.

Andrusha has disappeared. Doctor Tahabat is calmly sitting on the sofa and drinking wine. He silently follows my commands, and from time to time casts ironical glances at the portrait of the prince. But I feel these glances upon myself, and they weary and frustrate me.

The sun is setting. The evening is dying away. Night is drawing on. People are seen running to and fro on the ramparts, and the machine-gun rattles monotonously. The deserted chambers of the princes have grown dead with expectation.

I look at the doctor and cannot bear his glances at the ancient portrait. I say sharply: "Doctor Tahabat! In an hour I must liquidate the last party of the condemned. I must take a detachment."

Then he, ironically and indifferently: "Why, of course!" I grow restless, but the doctor looks at me and smiles. O, undoubtedly he understands what is the matter! Why, my mother is among those condemned to die.

I: "Please leave the room!"

The doctor: "Why, of course!"

At that I cannot restrain myself, and I fall into a rage; "Doctor Tahabat! For the last time I warn you: do not jest with me!" But my voice breaks, and I feel a babbling in my throat. I make an effort to seize my gun and immediately settle accounts with the doctor, but suddenly I feel so piteous and insignificant, and find that the remaining particles of my will are leaving me. I sit down on the sofa and piteously, like a beaten dog, look at Tahabat. But the minutes are passing away. We must be leaving.

Again I try to control myself, and for the last time I look at the portrait of the princess.

Darkness.

"Convoy!"

The sentinel appears and reports: "The party has been taken out. The execution is to be carried out beyond the city: where the pine forest begins."

From behind the distant mountain peaks the moon is rising. She drifts down the calm azure streams, shedding about her lemon-colored spray. At midnight she pierces the zenith and finds herself above a chasm.

A lively firing is going forward in the city.

We take the northern road.

I shall never forget this silent procession—the somber crowd being led to execution.

The wagon-trains are creaking behind me.

In front—the escorting communards, next—the crowd of nuns, in the rear—I, still more escorting communards, and doctor Tahabat.

But these are genuine Versaillais: during the entire progress not a single nun speaks a single word. They are quite sincere, these fanatics.

I walk down the road, as before—to nowhere in particular, while at my side move the sentinels of my soul: the doctor and the degenerate. I look at the crowd, but I see nothing there.

Instead I feel: There walks my mother with her head bent.

I can feel the scent of mint. I caress her dear head sprinkled with silvery grey.

Suddenly there rises before me the intangible distance. Once more, painfully, I feel like falling to my knees and looking pleadingly at the crude silhouette of the dark tribunal of the Commune.

I press my head with my hands and continue down the lifeless road, while behind me creak the wagon-trains.

Suddenly I am roused: "What is it? A hallucination? Is it really the voice of my mother?"

And again I feel insignificant, and somewhere under my heart I grow faint. I want to weep, not to wail, but to weep with down-dropping tears, just as I did in my childhood, on a warm breast.

It flashes through my mind: "Am I really leading her to execution?"

Which is it: reality or hallucination?

But it is reality: a veritable, vital reality—savage and cruel, like a pack of hungry wolves. It is a reality as irrevocable, as imminent as death itself.

But perhaps it is a mistake?

Perhaps something else should be done?

Ah, this is cowardly, vacillating. For is there not a certain law of life: *errare humanum est?* Why worry then? Err! and err precisely thus and not otherwise! And, after all, what are the mistakes you are apt to make?

Indeed: it is reality, and it is like a pack of hungry wolves. But still it is the only way to the distant lakes of the unknown and wonderful Commune.

And then I burn in the fire of fanaticism, and my

steps sound clearly on the northern road.

The silent procession approaches the pine forest. I do not remember how the nuns were stationed, I remember only the doctor coming up to me and placing his hand on my shoulder: "Your mother is there! Do as you please!"

I look:

From out of the throng a shape detaches itself, and lonely and silent moves towards the forest.

The moon is at its zenith, hanging over a chasm. The lifeless road withdraws into the green lemon-colored unknown. To the right the sentinel detachment of my battalion can be seen. And heavy firing rises above the city at this moment—the shots again sounding the alarm. The insurgents are withdrawing —the enemy has noticed this. A shell explodes to one side of us.

I take my pistol out of its leather case and hastily walk to the solitary shape. Just then, I remember, short fires were flashing: the nuns were being done away with.

Then, as I recall further—an armored train suddenly sounded the alarm from the pine forest. The forest resounded.

Fire flashes—once,

twice,

and again, and again!

The enemy regiments press on. I must hurry. Ah, I must hurry! But I move on and on, while the solitary shape of my mother is still in the distance. She stands, her arms outstretched, and looks sorrowfully at me. I hasten towards this enchanted, intolerable edge of the forest, while the solitary shape is still in the distance.

It is empty round about. Only the moon pours her green light down from the pierced zenith. In my hand I hold the pistol, but my hand is weakening, and I am on the point of bursting into thick-falling tears, as in my childhood days, upon a warm breast. I make an attempt to cry out: "Mother! Come to me, I tell you; for I must kill you!"

And the sorrowful voice again slashes my brain. Again I hear my mother say that I (her rebellious son) have completely tortured myself to death.

What is it? Is it really a hallucination? I throw my head back.

Yes, it was a hallucination: I stood long on the deserted edge of the forest, facing my mother and looking at her.

She was silent.

The armored train was clamoring in the forest. The fires were rising. The storm was approaching. The enemy attack began. The insurgents were withdrawing.

Then, in a daze, enveloped with the flames of an intolerable joy, I put my arm around my mother's neck and pressed her head to my breast. Then I raised my pistol and pressed the barrel to her temple.

Like a mown spike of wheat she fell on me.

I put her on the ground and looked wildly around. The space around me was deserted. To one side lay the black bodies of the nuns. The cannon was roaring nearby.

I put my hand in my pocket and immediately remembered that I had forgotten something in the halls of the princes.

"What a fool!" I thought. Then, glancing about: "Where are the people?" But I must hurry to my battalion! And I set off to regain the road.

But I had hardly taken three steps when something stopped me. I shuddered and ran to the body of my mother. I went down on my knees before it and stared at the face. But it was lifeless. Down the cheek, I remember, the blood was trickling in a dark stream.

Then I raised her helpless head and passionately glued my lips to her white forehead. Darkness.

Suddenly I heard: "Well, communard, get up! Time to join the battalion!"

I glanced round and saw the degenerate standing before me again.

"Oh, yes, I will. I will. I should have done that long ago!" Then I fixed the strap of my pistol and darted off to regain the road. In the steppe, the mounted insurgents were standing like distant knights of old. I ran in that direction, pressing my head with my hands.

The storm was approaching. Faint blots of dawn were to be seen here and there. The moon was silently fading away in the pierced zenith. The clouds were scudding over from the west. A sharp exchange of fire was going on.

I stopped in the midst of the lifeless steppe: there, in the distant unknown, most strangely glowed the peaceful lakes of the Commune beyond the hills.

———

Translated by C. H. Andrusyshyn.

A SENTIMENTAL TALE

The window was as black as ink, but a silent provincial dawn was already probing the dark gardens.

"Well, it's time," I thought and went out.

A carriage was waiting near the porch, the horse neighing faintly.

Mother wept, saying that I was treating her abominably. Why should I go to a strange place? Why? She had passed her whole life in the shelter of the four walls of our immaculate white cottage, and everything beyond the Zahaday bridge was to her a black and dreadful enigma. I kissed mother, telling her that in spite of everything I could not, somehow, stay. Did she not realize that the distance was luring me? Did she really think this was self-deception? I remember hugging her and groaning: "Darling! Darling!" My mother looked at me with fear in her eyes, soothing me. And I laughed aloud and kissed her again. Then I picked a bunch of flowers from our modest garden and sat down in the waiting carriage . . . A golden rooster flew up to the weather-vane, crowing loudly. The tiny cottage, the porch, and my mother gazed at me in sorrow. I told the driver to start. Then I fell back on the fresh fragrant hay and said to myself: "Forever!" I bit my lip so painfully that the tears rolled down my cheeks. But I had to make this journey.

My childhood was full of presentiments and vague terrors. When I was about six, I used to make my mother take me to church so that I could sit in a corner and listen intently to the vague, mysterious murmur. My grandmother used to tell me stories of the catacombs, and I used to imagine I was standing there.

I loved the meadows, the scent of the sedge and the green sea of grass plashing beyond the river; I had a passionate love for the snowdrifts in the evening, the reddish willows, and the thin smoke above the village. But I hated the people of the village so backward and savage with the savagery of the Tamerlane era, I yearned continually for the unknown, lost in distant lands.

Then I suddenly realized (my brother had died long ago on the barricades) a new savagery had arrived and that our land was ringing with the mechanized violence of Asiatic wildness, and only rarely young, faint winds blew through it. Then I began to believe that, somewhere, different people must live, and I was intolerably drawn towards them.

Obviously, this strengthened my desires to fly away; besides, the cranes had just brought me my seventeenth spring. At night I would go into the garden and even then I could not listen in peace to their clamour. That spring overwhelmed me, as if I were a swallow and had to fly somewhere beyond the sea.

I did not look back and did not see (so the driver told me) my mother waving a white kerchief after me, nor did I see (the driver told me) the sexton passing and looking at me in astonishment.

With the crowing of the rooster still ringing in my ears, the horse trotted briskly along, stirring the dust on the road.

We had long ago passed the office of the District Executive Committee and had left the Komsomol Club behind us. As I thought of it I sighed. I used to avoid this place as if I had escaped something. The way to the Komsomol had lain open to me, but I simply refused to belong. They hated me for this, because they knew why I hung back. I withdrew because I remembered the Komsomols who had lost lives in the civil war, and often, secretly, I used to honor these unknown heroes. But here, in our own Komsomol, such wild looseness reigned that the young girls who went there became, even at the age of fifteen, "respectable donors," as they were called. I talked about it openly, and they called me a reactionary. I remember that once a communist, who had arrived unexpectedly in our town, remonstrated with them: "What's the matter, young fellows," he said, "isn't she telling the truth?"

The green glade of the distant forest bore down upon us. Alongside, the golden, eternally strange sun was already stretching out its crimson wings. Suddenly we slowed down: in front of us moved a herd of sheep, a shepherd following them. The shepherd played something melancholy and I felt even sadder. I whistled and told the driver faster, and the horse trotted on once more. The morning wind rushed after him.

"Trot-trot-trot!" I cried out.

I bared my young breasts to the wind, and the wind caressed them. I laughed and laughed all the way to the station. But I could not tell the driver why. It was because I wanted to be a mother, and the wind made me restless. I wanted (how ridiculous!) to become pregnant by it. I wanted to become as absolutely pregnant as the light-blue sky which, for millions of ages now, had concealed within itself the mystery of the loveliest and most immaculate conception. This wild fantasy would not give me peace and kept me in a state of terror all the way. The fields rushed away and the Swedish hillocks[1] looked austere as they passed us. I thought of Maria Kochubey.[2]

We arrived at the station after darkness had fallen. I bought a ticket, kissed the driver (how surprised he was) and took my small belongings from the carriage.

"Now it really is forever," it dawned upon me, for the driver was the last, the closest being to me. Then, as never before, I felt the great pain of parting, and just because this pain was great and unaffected, I felt myself to be the sincerest of all human beings. "A calf, of course, is not capable of experiencing this," I thought beginning to philosophize. Naturally, it was a terribly naive philosophy, for at that time I was acquainted (and superficially at that) only with Plato. But it did me no harm, indeed it

---

[1] Graves of the soldiers of the Swedish army which was defeated in the Ukraine (1709) by Peter I of Russia.

[2] Maria Kochubey was in love with the Cossack Hetman, Mazepa, who joined Charles XII of Sweden in the war against Russia.

was the only way to comfort myself.

The driver had long ago disappeared behind the hillocks while I still stood staring after him. It was half an hour before I returned to myself. I had to put an end to it, and I did: I made a gesture of renunciation and entered the dark silhouette of the station.

Dull as hundreds of other stations in the steppe, the station was littered with strangers. It smelled faintly of something sticky, for about nine versts away there was, I think, a sugar factory. When autumn comes, I thought, the girls would go to work on the beet plantations. And then the Poltava hillocks would grieve, and my memories roamed through the mirage of ages, and passed beyond the Executive Committee Building, beyond the Komsomol meadows. And such thoughts must come to all, it seemed, who have known the cherry-eyed Ukraine—that fantastic land of wild and somber paths that lead to the romantic Commune. And again I thought of Maria Kochubey.

Then I stepped on to the deserted track, gazed at the rails, at the green lights, sensed a darkening. Somebody walked past me (the stationmaster, I suppose) and looked attentively into my eyes. Then the train came flying in from the steppe, roaring, steaming, clamoring. Once more I looked at the steppe, where our white cottage stood, a rooster perched on the vane, where lay our modest grove and the gloomy provincial gardens. But I did not want to be reminded of anything and boarded the train. That which had been must vanish forever. See it once more? No! No! No! Not until the train had roared into motion did I, for the last time, take leave of the twilit steppe station. The outline of the buildings sped before my eyes and disappeared. I did not even think of coming back. Life was wide and boundless, my existence short as the beak of a sparrow.

"Tra-ta-ta!" the wheels clattered.

At night a candle flickered, the passengers droned away somewhere, the train was rocking, but I could not fall asleep. During the day the fields rushed by and the tumuli flew past, but they interested me no longer. I remember how my thoughts jostled foolishly all the way: they rushed madly, tumbling over one another. This must have been reflected in my face, and people looked at me with astonishment.

On the third day I arrived at Z.

II

Leaving the station, I was immensely happy. I looked at the window displays, the buses, the streetcars, and heard people say: "Look, what a peasant!"

I walked down a big street and suddenly found myself in a market square. There were women with strawberries. The strawberries smelled so sweet that straightaway I bought two pounds of them. Then, for a long time I wandered about the city, until the blue urban evening took me by surprise. I remember taking one juicy berry out of the bag and putting it between my lips. I took it carelessly, for the juice trickled down, making a rosy spot on my blouse.

As the evening deepened, the prostitutes came out. They quarrelled so fearfully that several times I blushed to the tips of my ears. And I would never have found Lisbeth in this city had it not been for an accident.

There was a summer garden near an advertisement sign. A boy leaped, yelling, straight at my face. . . . Then the carriages began to roll up, lights flashed, and the evening sky became very, very blue. I went to the summer garden, ate five kopeks worth of ice-cream, and then turned into the alley of the "Blue Tavern." There I met Lisbeth. Along the road she patted me on the back saying "How nice, how nice of you to have come!"

I had been friendly with Lisbeth ever since our schooldays, and had never lost touch with her. She was very fond of me. She worked as a typist, and promised to find a job for me in her office.

But how could she do it, when I knew nothing at all about that kind of work? Lisbeth laughed and told me that in a month I would be a first-rate typist. I was surprised to see how quickly this happened and we put it down to my unusual abilities. Meanwhile, Lisbeth winked slyly and said that first I must go and visit the office for a while. "What for?" I asked. She laughed again and called me naive. Did I not yet know that my face would launch a thousand ships? Lisbeth took out a mirror and told me to look at myself. I was horrified: did she really want me to sell my body? But she assured me there was no question of selling; they would only look at me, that was all. I agreed, and got the job. A week or two later Lisbeth went away to visit her aunt, and left me her apartment. "Well, good-bye," she said, "Perhaps we'll meet again one day."

The window of my room opened from the basement into a small courtyard where stood an old green summer house. I would sit near it and look at a patch of blue sky which appeared so remarkable there, as if nature had concentrated all her joy into that tiny corner. I thought of that strange distance which had drawn me out of my native land and which was still so far away, ah, so far away! Certainly I did not expect to find it in Z, but I thought that there I might meet a great man, and then a miracle would happen.

Sometimes after work I would not go back home, but would wander wherever fancy led. Then people looked as if I were crazy. I would go to the northeastern outskirts of the city, where humble houses in narrow ravines pressed close to each other. Beacons flickered in the steppe, and night drew on. I would stop on a hillock dreaming of the Niebelungenlied and of Siegfried. Then I would gaze, gazing for a long time as if some unknown power were moving upon me. After a few hours of this, I would go home, and lie down on my bed for a long time with my eyes closed. In the city tower the clock would strike: "Clang! Clang!"

To all appearances I was lonely in the office, but to tell the truth the typewriter was my only friend. I used to love it so much that I even dreamed of it, that it was a living creature and could answer all my questions in a warm, beautiful voice. I dreamed that when I lowered my head on to the keys, the roller murmured softly to me. The keys rose and clattered sorrowfully, like a train flying into an unknown land. Once more I saw the road, the steppe, and the fragrant russet hedges. "Ah, my dear friend," I used to say, taking out some note for Kuk, the manager.

Kuk was the manager who employed me. He was very quiet, wore a very neat suit, and always had a straight part in his hair. It was hard to distinguish him from a Gogolian hero. He signed his papers legibly, the last letter of his name trailing into a downward flourish like a blossom. Before stamping his seal on this or that paper he would rub his hands passionately and make a queer satisfied cluck with his tongue. His nose was unusually large and anyway did not suit his small face. He was obviously an elderly roué, and had a passion for young typists. He would sidle up to me and roll his leaden eyes. This made him look like a monkey, a fact of which he was quite unconscious. He was quite without culture and talked grotesquely, as if he were imitating someone.

"How delightful," he would often say, "to walk in the park with a beautiful girl, you, for example, and to feel that she is worthy of one."

That manikin's vulgarity was so unpleasant to listen to that I would make any excuse to get out of his way.

But then in the corridor I would meet, without fail, the grey-eyed journalist. She was a fairly attractive woman, but she would never leave my hands alone. Passing by, she would stop at my desk and ask in a whisper if I would allow her to 'pinch' her dear Bianca once more. Naturally I would not, but all the same, there were several blue marks on my hand, and there was even a blue mark on my right breast. She was certainly a sadist, and a few months later I became convinced of it. "I shall be compelled," I told her once, "to complain to the local committee."

She laughed, as if to say, "Go ahead, I've always known you were a slanderer" (that's what she said, 'slanderer') . . . . And what could I have said to that?

So there was only one person with whom I felt more or less at ease. That was Comrade Ulyana, a communist and wife of a former communist, Comrade B. She lived in the same building as I, and when I returned home she would knock at my door and ask if she might come in. I would say "Certainly!" and in she would come. Right from the beginning she started to tell me that she had a very ugly face. I understood her and always tried to calm her, telling her that it was nothing of the kind, that she was not as ugly as she thought. I told her, for example, that her hair was very lovely and that her eyes were good. Comrade Ulyana did not agree and argued hotly. She used killing arguments and slew me with them mercilessly. So in the end the impression was created that I was defending not her but myself, and that it was I who was ugly and not she.

Comrade Ulyana was waiting for a miracle, but this miracle never did and never will happen. She was a cultured person, realistic about her face and figure (my neighbor was a tall, thin pike of a woman with a broken nose). But to me she disclosed her soul, and I helped her. I learned that Comrade Ulyana lived on bad terms with her husband, but she never spoke to me about Comrade B.

"Poor Comrade B!" would on very rare occasions burst from her, and then she would sigh deeply.

With Comrade Ulyana the circle of my acquaintances closed. All these people were, I thought, so petty and in one way or another on a level with myself and thus unable to help me out of that enchanted circle of savagery which obstructed my view of those mysterious regions far away.

Once, after work, the manager approached me and began to talk me into going to dinner with him. He said "Whereas" (that is what he said—"Whereas") he had been advanced some money, and "whereas" that day was the anniversary of his birth, he would like to take a walk down the boulevard with me, and drink a bottle of beer. I agreed, and we went. We went to a beer-parlor and sat down at a table. There was noise and smoke in the bar. It smelled of intoxication. The odor was sharp, charred, and at once went to one's head. The orchestra was playing something ribald from some comic operetta. We drank two bottles. The manager began kissing my elbow and telling me about his unhappy life. His misery consisted in the fact that officials hardly noticed him and would not promote him, and "whereas" he wanted to be general manager, such a "check" to his career could not but alarm him. He even wept a little, and I felt sorry for him.

"Ah, Bianca!" he continued, "how wonderful is life, if a wide career stretches before one, and one could become general manager of Radnarkom."[3]

The manager pronounced this in such eloquent and pathetic accents, that I felt even more sorry for him. He kissed my elbow again and assured me that he loved only me. Kuk spoke of love quite seriously, as if I had some interest in it.

We had already drunk more than enough, and the

---

[3] Council of People's Commissars.

manager asked me to take him home. With all his lack of brains he always managed to survive by his low cunning; he knew that the beer had made him drunk, and that if unsupported he would be tipsy. Hanging on to my arm, however, he was not afraid to compromise himself. I agreed—and we went.

On the way, we passed through a park and there sat down on a bench. A man was sitting to one side of us. I glanced at him. He had worried and (I thought) lovely eyes. He sat like a statue looking somewhere into the sky. Suddenly Kuk rose, tugged at his jacket as if he were going to make an official report, and turned to the stranger. "If you will permit me to ask you: you are, I think, the artist, Charhar?"

"Yes, I am—Charhar, the artist," said the man, in a soft and pleasant baritone such as I had only read of in romantic novels. "What can I do for you?"

I shuddered. And how could I not shudder? I was fortunate enough to be sitting beside a painter renowned in our country. The presence of an artist moved me so much that I immediately blushed and felt my ears burning.

Charhar turned his head and looked closely at me. He may have glanced at me in a quite ordinary way, but I could not stand it, and lowered my eyelids.

Kuk said that he had known the artist for a long time, and for quite a while had wished to acquaint himself with the subject (that is what he said—"subject") of the incomparable Charharian pictures. The artist corrected him: "Perhaps you mean 'with the creator'?" The manager said that he had meant what he said "subject."

Then we lapsed into silence and looked at the wires flashing blue flames (a streetcar was flying along just after the rain had stopped). A siren screamed out somewhere. Kuk slipped side-ways and began to doze. Then the artist said: "Have I the honor of speaking to the manager's wife?"

"You have the honor of speaking to one who is not the manager's wife at all," I said, and laughed.

A few moments of unusual inner tension were released into an almost hysterical laugh. I giggled quite foolishly (obviously, I was encouraged by the beer), but Charhar showed not the slightest sign of considering me a nitwit. Then once more he looked closely at me and said: "You know, it didn't even dawn upon me that such wonderful women existed in our city."

"Is that so?" I asked and blushed again, for that was the greatest praise anyone could have given my body.

After that, I thought only of how I could return the compliment to Charhar. He smiled, and said that he was terribly pleased with my simplicity and spontaneity. For, in our hypocritical age, it was very rare and, if you please, even bad taste. He was tall and straight, with a close-shaven, swarthy face, wearing an ordinary shirt a la Tolstoy, and without any claims to distinction. All the time he was looking around him rather aimlessly.

Then it began to grow dark, and the evening news was flashed on the street screen. The sky became deep blue. The manager snored. I called a coachman, took his number, gave him the address of Kuk's apartment, and the coachman took the manager home. I did all this without looking behind me. But my heart was beating so fast that I was certain that the artist was standing somewhere there waiting for me.

I was not mistaken: he was standing there. Then I went up to him, as if we were old friends, and he offered me his arm. I took it and we walked down the path. Charhar wanted to know who I was. I told him. Then we left the park and walked down the avenue of the Rebellion. We reached the Radnarkom and stopped. A red army sentinel stood near the door in a sentry box. He stood like a statue, and Charhar said: "Doesn't he remind you of anything?" I said he did. Then, for some reason, Charhar smiled. I asked why, but he did not answer, and suddenly held out his hand to me. We parted: I went in one direction, he in the opposite.

I came home with the feeling I had in my childhood, coming back from early service on Easter morning. The world seemed so lovely and rosy that I was ready to run out into the street and kiss the first person I met. "My dear, my handsome!" cried my entire being, "it was only you I needed."

It was dawn when I fell asleep; all night I was wondering where I would meet Charhar again.

III

Our meeting had been quite accidental, and I felt almost certain that such an accident would not happen again. It could not happen again, because he must already have forgotten me. Charhar must have met many a woman like me, I reflected, in his time.

Once, I left the office and wandered about the city for several hours. I wandered aimlessly, and came to the place where I had parted from Charhar; I paused. To my right stood the dark outline of a synagogue, and above it broken clouds were pierced by a horn of the crescent moon. The violet sidewalk advertisements were reflected at my feet. Suddenly somebody from behind seized my hands. I turned, and saw the grey-eyed journalist. "Good evening," she said, "at last I've met you on the street. I thought you never went anywhere."

"That's too bad," I said, "but I go to the city gardens almost every evening."

"Well, well! And I didn't know."

Then she told me that devils bred in a quiet mudhole, that . . . etc. I told her that "devils" had nothing to do with me, for I went out alone and did not know any men. The grey-eyed journalist fiddled with her hat and drawled: "What is this? Does a universal grief gnaw your heart? Or perhaps, a highfalutin' loneliness won't allow you to rest?"

Suddenly she spat. Was it just a gesture, or a sign of real resentment? I do not know even now. In any case, this spitting through her teeth seemed quite out of character. Naturally I did not tell her that, but only screwed up my face a little.

She did not stop, but went on with her romancing. She talked of the white St. Petersburg nights, and of the passion that boils then. These nights intrigued her most when youths with calculating eyes wandered up and down the Nevsky Prospekt selling their bodies.

I was surprised: did young men sell their bodies?

The grey-eyed journalist laughed and gritted her teeth. Then she told me that it was quite the usual thing, and she was very surprised there were none to be found in our city. They would earn a good deal: for would not she, for example, buy them?

"But only a rotten person is capable of such licentiousness," I said.

"Quit stringing me (that is what she said—"stringing me"), we know you innocent ones: you say one thing and do something completely different; in any case they cannot take us to the com-cell!"

"What has the com-cell got to do with this?" and I smiled.

She answered at random. Then she returned to the old subject and again wearied me with assurances that young men were right to sell their bodies. If fortune should ever make her rich, she would make it a point to employ pages.

The journalist talked to me so cynically that I began to doubt whether she was in her right mind. She told me a great deal, but, when I tried to go and said I had no time, she suddenly yawned and in a completely different tone came out with: "How naive you are, Bianca, really! Can't you see that the earth has been rolling into an abyss for quite a long time now, and that we are on the eve of a universal catastrophe? Can't you?"

I looked at her. She was gazing dreamily at the sky and seemed to be talking to herself. "Ah, what a short while still remains for us to live! Don't you feel that the earth is gradually becoming colder?" She shuddered as if she were really cold. I did not know what to say, so I kept quiet.

"Perhaps a glacial period is approaching. Perhaps something else. How wonderful it would be if we were to become gods! Don't you think?"

Then suddenly she suggested I should go with her to a brothel, and when I refused, she spat through her teeth again and left without saying a word.

A streetcar flew past, next a bus came dashing by, and I heard a scream: the bus had crushed a child. A mother had been walking along, had become frightened, and had let her child drop from her arms. Then the bus came rushing madly—and what had been a child was now a carcass. The mother went out of her mind and was taken to the hospital. Further on, the evening star appeared, flickering above the city hall, and the buildings melted into a darkening distance. A straight street set out from the clubhouse of the Association of Soviet Sanitationists.

I went further and stopped, for no reason at all, at a Japanese tavern: a fantastic lamp was hanging above the door, and a mechanical Japanese girl was inviting guests inside.

Suddenly I shuddered: someone again took my elbow. I turned round and saw Charhar. I turned very pale, for he was looking at me with his wonderful eyes, and saying: "What is the matter with you? Why is your face so pale?"

I told him that he was simply imagining it, for I was quite well. He said that he had been wanting to see me for quite a while now, but that he had not known my address.

"Is that so?" I asked.

He began to upbraid me hotly, saying that there

was no reason for me to doubt him—during the past few days he had thought only of how he could meet me. For he had been moved by my "saintly" (that is what he said, "saintly") simplicity.

Charhar told me other things too, but that was enough. With boundless gratitude I looked at the artist.

We went down into the cellar. As we were going down the steps Charhar took my arm. We were met by an Armenian. I laughed and asked what was the sense in calling this a Japanese tavern. The Armenian did not answer and showed us to a private compartment. While supper was being prepared, we waited in the public hall where a gypsy was playing a fiddle and a prostitute was dancing. Charhar threw a few silver coins to the gypsy, and he played something from "The Corsair."

All that evening I laughed and drank brandy. We sat in the compartment for two hours. Charhar stroked my fingers and said he liked my hand, especially since my nails were cut short unlike those of modern girls. "Long nails," he said, "symbolize something ferocious and profligate." Then he damped his handkerchief in a glass of wine and, smiling, asked to be allowed "to verify my face." I let him and he realized that I did not use make-up. He talked about virginity and finally turned his talk on to mine. "I am not mistaken, am I?" he asked.

"You are not mistaken," I said, understanding at once what he was driving at. Then he told how innocence moved him, not in the sense that at the thought of it the male within him was aroused, but that the artist awakened inside him.

We drank to our friendship. He ordered a bottle of champagne, and when we left the tavern I was tipsy. Charhar put his hand round my waist, and I looked intently into his eyes. His eyes were shining, with depths in them to drive one mad. "Charhar," I said, "we have met quite accidentally. But don't you think this is . . ." I could not find the right word and paused. Then he said: "Fate"—and I understood him.

"Haven't you ever been tortured by the mystery of Distance?" I asked abruptly.

He was silent. I asked him again. He removed his hand from my waist and said somewhat reluctantly: "I don't understand you!"

"You don't understand me?" I asked in astonishment, for it had not occurred to me that Charhar might not understand. Then, somewhat incoherently, I tried to explain my thought. From abstraction I suddenly switched to concrete examples. On the one hand my Distance was postulated by certain social inter-relations, on the other—it remained aloof and detached from life and all commonplace interests. For the first time I had had to answer a direct question, and not until then did I realize what an endlessly intricate problem stood before me. It upset me a little, but, on the other hand, a desire to fathom this mysterious Distance inflated me with still greater passion.

"Obviously, I am speaking incoherently," I said, "but it is impossible for you not to understand me. Listen: please give yourself up to intuition, and everything will become clear to you."

"It is already clear to me!" Charhar said suddenly.

"In other words, it had tortured you too?"

He was about to answer me, but suddenly flung back his hair and changed the subject. I felt him grow cold and asked why he refused to answer me. Charhar grew more austere and was silent all the way. I thought that perhaps I had been very unconventional in my behavior. After all, it was only our second meeting, and in any case I had no right to be so importunate. I wanted to ask his forgiveness, but could not, and only pressed close to the artist. He, naturally, understood me and took my hand. He stroked it in silence all the way.

When we drew near to my street the flares in the airfields moved and suddenly flashed skywards. The sky glowed like an agate. A quail cried out somewhere. In the garden of the Parisian Communards sky-rockets were being sent up. They pierced the sky with their red tails and scattered into millions of stars.

At last we approached the building in which I lived. Charhar pressed my hand and said, a little coldly: "Au revoir!"

"Well, then let it be 'au revoir'!" I did not then attach much importance to this coolness. But when I was left alone I began to wonder why he had said goodbye so coldly. Perhaps Charhar wanted to see in me only a naive girl and my questions made him nervous. Then again it occurred to me that an artist guards somewhat jealously the approaches to his inner world. This assumption seemed the most likely when I thought over our conversation. "Well, good," I reflected, "guard them! But you will not succeed, for you have already given me the right to treat you familiarly."

One day, Comrade Ulyana came to see me. She was terribly upset, and there were dark rings under her eyes. We sat down on the sofa and began to talk. At first we talked about the theater (I do not exactly remember what), and then Comrade Ulyana suddenly said: "I envy you terribly, Bianca, and not because you are beautiful. Guess why?"

I had been talking somewhat mechanically about the theater, agreeing with everything she said (I was thinking of my next meeting with Charhar) and so I said rather shortly: "I don't know."

Comrade Ulyana went up to the mirror and began to fix her hair. It was a dull day, and grey clouds were passing over the sky, so that it had grown quite dark in my room. On the opposite side, at the Jewish tailor's a lamp had even been lighted.

I looked at Comrade Ulyana; her forehead was pale and she was smiling. She smiled so unpleasantly that I probably looked frightened. She asked why I was afraid.

"You looked at me so queerly," I said.

"Nothing of the kind!" said Comrade Ulyana sharply, clutching nervously at her broken nose. "I looked at you quite ordinarily. But why won't you let me finish?"

I realized that Comrade Ulyana had asked me a question and that I had not treated it considerately. Then I begged her pardon and told her that I had felt a little scatter-brained lately.

"I envy you," she said, "I envy you because you belong to the new generation, and because to you our worries are meaningless."

"If you think so, you are mistaken," I said.

"Don't speak! You have never been on the other side of the river, and you know nothing. Only we were there, and only we have been driven from there. And now we roam about, grieving. Heavens! you cannot imagine what a wonderful country it is. Under its sun not only the inner world of each one of us was transformed and we were made ideal, but we were physically born anew. I swear to you! Even physically we were ideal men and women."

Comrade Ulyana sighed deeply. It was quite dim in my room, but I saw that her face was shining with the brightness of an extraordinary joy. She was silent for a long time, until the children made an outcry behind the window, when she said, shuddering: "Of course, you won't believe me when I say that I was beautiful several years ago—I know that! But, believe me, at least Comrade B. loved me. I swear to you he did: he loved me so . . . he loved me so . . ."

Comrade Ulyana suddenly leaned over the back of the sofa and wept softly. It was quiet everywhere (only the spaniel at the dentist's yelped mournfully) and her lamentations rent the air as dully as if she were in her coffin.

I tried to soothe her. But she would not be consoled for a long time, and it was half an hour before I heard Ulyana beg me, through her tears, not to pay any attention to her, she always felt better after weeping. She even smiled, and that smile was so childlike, so innocent, that I went down on my knees in front of her and said quite seriously: "Comrade Ulyana, I swear to you that I have never seen you like this: today you shine with an unearthly beauty like

Raphael's Madonna."

But she was silent. I lowered my head to her torn shoes and remained motionless there. I embraced her legs and kissed them passionately. I was enveloped by an almost religious feeling of charity towards this small human suffering. And, if at that moment, Comrade Ulyana had wished to lead me to death, I would have gone without a shudder.

Then a cricket began to chirp and a piercing siren clamored, long and drawn out. Behind the window the tailor's boy was crying, and the Jew was vociferating dully. Comrade Ulyana rose. She took my head between her hands and kissed it. She kissed it so that even now I can feel a shiver creep up my back. Then she left me.

Suddenly I burst into tears. They were the first tears I shed in this big city.

IV

I used to meet Charhar frequently, but did not enter his apartment until three months after we had met. I had never imagined how poorly such a famous artist lived. His room, like mine, was underground. The walls smelled like a cave, and there was a continual rusty patch of damp on his ceiling. Just above his room there was a Soviet Employees Club, and so his ceiling was always trembling with stamping and noise. Charhar told me that he had already complained several times to the officials, but—in short, he would obviously never move. I said it might have been better to speak to the chairman of the Executive Committee, but as I said it I made a gesture indicating the uselessness of the attempt. He did the same, and we both laughed.

I remember that I took off my jacket, fixed my hair, and began to look over the heavy volumes scattered in disorder about the room. A sunbeam peeped through the window and its reflection played on the wall. Charhar sat facing his easel looking attentively at the canvas. I asked if he would like to paint my body. I would willingly pose for him. He said that that was quite unnecessary, it was not in his line. "I have never painted women yet, and probably never will paint them."

I asked him why. He did not answer. Just then a heavy book drew my attention: it was a dissertation on Swedish tumuli. The artist noticed it, and said that for several years he had been preoccupied with the idea of producing a large canvas upon which Charles XII and Mazepa would flee after the defeat.[4] He hoped to create a picture of universal importance.

On the whole, Charhar spoke little. Phrases would tear themselves away from him rather abruptly, as if he were really abnormal. But this time he came out with a complete story. True, he spoke terribly incoherently and vaguely, but I was satisfied even with that: I was able to guide our intimacy to the utmost limit, and resolved to take him by storm. He held my hand, kissing my fingers. But his kisses were cold and numb.

---

[4] The battle of Poltava was fought in 1709 between the forces of Peter I and those of Charles XII, assisted by Mazepa. Peter's victory put an end to the hopes for Ukrainian independence from Russia.

"Well, here you are kissing my hands," I said, "but what on earth do you call these kisses?"

"What do you mean?" asked Charhar.

"I mean, are these the kisses you would use (I purposely said 'use') when meeting the woman you love?"

He shrugged and looked at me with astonishment: as if to say he deliberately refused to understand me.

"Pardon! But I think what I said was clear," and I moved the easel away from him.

Charhar jumped nervously and rather feebly answered me with a thin, polite laugh. "You know, let's not talk about these things!"

This made me lose my temper and I said quite sharply: "Well, if it were a question of love, would you tell them the same thing even then?"

He looked at me dejectedly and said, in a scarcely audible voice, "I don't know how to love." His soft, pleasant baritone seemed lost, and he spoke in an almost childish soprano. Just at that moment, and for the first time, something close to hatred for him was roused within me.

"That's all right," I said, "I don't even want you to love me, I dare not even dream of it. But at least allow me to love you."

He again laughed a small laugh, and suddenly, transfigured, said sternly: "Isn't it time we stopped talking about this?"

"You think so?" I asked, "Well, and if . . . I wanted to give myself to you, would you take me?"

This last phrase escaped me somewhat unexpectedly. I had never reached such a cynical state before, but just then a presentiment of something extraordinary, something which terrified me all of a sudden with a frightful power, might have thrust me yet further.

"Suppose we drop that subject for today?" asked Charhar coldly.

I thought he accented 'today' and I asked "Then perhaps you will let me come to you tomorrow?"

Charhar did not answer, but closed his eyes. His face seemed almost dead, and I was frightened. Immediately, I became conscious of the horror of my situation. For I was such a marginal figure in the great artist's life. He had only to say 'enough' and I would never see him again. "Heavens!" I thought to myself, "what impudence! What gave me the right to treat him this way? For he must realize that my proposal is only one of the ways in which I am trying to bring him out to the light."

But another voice in my soul was devilishly whispering something quite different. I was saying to myself that I was not at all a casual figure in his life. For did I not possess all the attributes? Intellectually, I was quite a developed person; physically, I was considered a beauty; youth was on my side, and so was sexual innocence. And, after all, what does 'casual' mean? This word had already begun to make me nervous, for rather too suddenly I appreciated my own worth.

"That is, you want me to drop all this and keep quiet? Well, I am quiet."

"That's better!" he said and straightaway asked, "Will you have lunch with me?"

"Lunch? What a sudden change!" Well, I agreed, and we went out into the street.

In half an hour we were in the Karakadze restaurant. There we met a young composer. I was introduced to him (I have forgotten his name now). The composer suggested we go to the Zoological Gardens after lunch. He assured us we would not regret it: wonderful specimens had been brought there recently.

"I am rather surprised to find a composer so interested in zoology," I said.

"It is a little odd, but we cannot get along without nature study these days."

He said this ironically. But I did not understand him. "Only it's too bad that our worthy Charhar is not interested in science."

"Is that true?" I asked, turning to the artist.

Charhar regarded me sternly. The composer, who probably considered me Charhar's mistress, suddenly rose and bowed, as if to say that he was revoking his invitation because he did not want to be the cause of a family row.

When the composer had left us, I turned to Charhar—"Did you hear?" I said, "He is quite certain that I am your mistress."

"And does it interest you so much?" asked Charhar in his usual cool, level voice.

"If it didn't interest me, I wouldn't talk about it," I said, realizing that an unspoken struggle had already begun between us.

I got up and went to the mirror. I knew my own worth, but I had never seen myself so beautiful before. Then I sensed that Charhar was conscientiously and unwillingly thrusting me away from him today. It was obvious that he was trying to prevent any further intimacy between us. For some reason he was afraid of it.

But I needed it as I needed air, for only thus could I reach that last nook of the human soul still unknown to me, in which the chimerical lakes of that enigmatic Distance must be most clearly reflected.

I said that I was going home; he offered to come with me. I refused. Then, the following conversation took place.

"No, don't bother. I'll go myself," I said, "but let me remind you that my frankness has pleased you —hasn't it, my frankness?"

"Well, yes," said Charhar.

"Of course, frankness. A philistine convention does not allow a woman to be the first to speak of love. I am quite outside this convention and so I can say—I love you madly."

"I know that," said Charhar coldly.

"And you, of course, know that I am a virgin?"

"I know that too."

"Well, I want you to be my first man. I want to give myself to you."

"I know that too," Charhar spoke coldly again.

"Then I must be physically repulsive to you?"

"Nothing of the kind," he blurted out, gritting his teeth.

It was terribly moving. In the middle of a noisy street a beautiful woman stood offering her body. People rushed past us and watched Charhar and me with astonishment. There flamed within me that feeling which players experience during a game. I said that I had to go to the library. Charhar offered to go with me. I did not refuse. But when we came to the door, it was locked. And I remembered that that was the librarians' day of rest.

"Will you let me come to you tomorrow?" I asked, looking at Charhar.

"I have already told you!"

"You mean you are not willing?"

"Yes!"

Then I pressed his hand and went home. I walked along, shuddering all the time as if I had a chill. It was impossible not to shudder, for it was the first time I had talked so cynically and frankly. "Like the grey-eyed journalist," I thought.

I remember that for the first time in my life I opened the Bible and began to read it carefully. I read almost all night. When I tore myself away from it, I saw before me the spotless cottage, the golden rooster perched on the vane, and the road leading to the flat steppe country. "My God, what have I come to! What is this? Why torture myself and someone else?" But simultaneously a voice whispered devilishly to me: "He knows everything, you must overcome him and take from him that without which you are nothing, without which you do not exist!"

It was, of course, a terrible romanticism, but even now I respect it. I respect it for its immovable will, for its manifestation of real human foolishness. The point is that I, as I later realized, bodily tried to oppose myself to my age, and my age mocked me. I wanted to unite the pure, the holy romanticism of my nature with the naked and soiled truth of life, but my desire was shattered on the blank wall of a manicured age. Even during that last meeting with Charhar I had an intuition that nothing could come of it, and that in this unequal struggle I should be demoralized, nothing more nor less. But all this was merely intuition, imperfectly understood; otherwise Charhar would not have loomed so large, in this dull wearisome, and commonplace world.

"Ah, you wretched Don Quixote," I thought of myself.

The core of the tragedy was that I was born into this age. There were times when I mocked myself. Then a powerful scepticism started to devour my faith—and broken pieces would be all that remained of my romanticism. At eighteen I already knew everything: the dull, provincial countryside and the life of the capital; and I even knew the way of life of that wonderful cemetery—decaying Europe. I could see no other roads. Return to the country I could not, and no Rousseau could have lured me back with his village idylls.

"Ah, you wretched Don Quixote!" I sighed once more.

A blue city night was moving past my window and the traditional carriages were clattering somewhere outside. Finally, I stopped reading the Bible and went to the wash basin. I cleaned my teeth, washed my breasts with cold water and went to bed. But even in bed I could not sleep for a long time.

During the night it rained. It thundered, and lightning seemed to cut the window of my cellar. I sat up in my bed looking at the green summerhouse. I thought of Turgeniev's women—so pure and lovely —and reflected that there would never be such women again, and even I, who knew not man, even I had long ago lost my purity.

Lightning was cutting the window-pane. I opened the window. A linden tree was blooming nearby, and it smelled of something beautiful and distant. The city slept, but I did not sleep that night.

V

I think, as I thoughtfully turn over the leaves of that time, a not altogether sorry human document emerges from my story. And I regret that I lack the elementary skill to coin a word.

Summer grew into autumn, and I saw Charhar only two or three times. And these meetings were terribly brief.

After I showed myself opposed to him, Charhar seemed to grow reserved and certainly avoided me. I had never gone to see him, of course, for my pride forbade it. But all the time I expected something to happen and so I lived continually in a state of vague anticipation.

Once the manager came up to me and, as usual, began to flatter me. He asked why I didn't go to the City Park any more. "Since," he said, "I would very much like to take a walk in that park with a beauty like you, near the bust of Karl Marx, for example."

I told him that I hardly ever went out and, to get rid of him, gave him a paper to sign. But the manager was still unwilling to end the conversation.

"What do you do after work?" he asked, "Read books? Why, it's enlightening! I like to read love stories myself (that is what he said—'love stories'). You know," he continued, enthusiastically, "it is so wonderful to lie on a bed, open a book and read!

About love and all kinds of adventures."

I certainly had no desire to listen to him so I told him I had no time, because there was still a great deal of work to be done. Then again he started inviting me to the park. "Do come!" he said, "there, for example, the flower of our city assembles. It's really a Bois de Boulogne (that is what he said—'Bois de Boulogne'). On the one hand, you see people such as commissars, and on the other, the pick of the artistic world. Recently, for example, I saw that artist —do you remember him?"

Suddenly my heart began to beat faster. For the past few days I had been wandering purposefully about the city in the hope of meeting Charhar. So when the manager told me that he had seen him in City Park, I at once decided to go there.

As soon as it grew dark, I hurried to the bus terminal. There I boarded a number six bus, and in half an hour found myself near the entrance to City Park.

A warm, transparent autumn was hovering. Couples rustled along the paths. Leaves were falling in the depths of the shrubbery. When I paused on a distant hillock, it looked as if an intermittent rain was falling. Then I saw the sky. It was of a crystalline purity and its soft turquoise caressed my eyes. Beyond the park, somewhere in the open fields, young women were singing. I thought of our provincial savagery and of the Swedish mounds. The moon was rising from behind the trees. I was frightened. The anticipation of meeting Charhar after such a long separation made my heart at once contract and beat faster. There were moments when it seemed that this evening might be my judgment day. When I look now over the road I have travelled, I realize that it was not so much the female that spoke with me. But that evening I thought that I only wanted to give myself to the artist. I wanted to put his head on my lap and caress it.

"What mad joy," I even whispered to myself, "to be his slave! What happiness to lie at his feet and feel oneself so small, so insignificant!"

It did not even occur to me to demand anything from him. His secrets I no longer needed, at least so I thought that evening. I was simply waiting for Charhar.

At that moment, as usual, I felt I had to laugh and whistle. I did whistle. Then I turned my hat inside out and put it on my head. I sat down on a bench. The grief of a violoncello came flying to me: there was a loudspeaker over the observatory, and the evening concerts were beginning. The violoncello's grief hovered over the park. Then I jumped up to leave, my patience had snapped. I wanted so much to see Charhar.

Just then, however, the figure of the manager appeared from behind a tree and stopped beside me. "Good evening," he said. I answered with disappointment. Kuk told me that he had been roaming about for quite a while and had not supposed that I was there too. Then he crooked his arm and suggested that I wander around with him. I wanted to refuse, but thought of our talk in the morning. So I went: I was afraid he might suspect my interest in Charhar.

"Are you by any chance thinking of getting married?" the manager asked me unexpectedly, and looked into my eyes.

"I like that!" I said ironically.

"What do you like?" Kuk did not understand me.

"That you start galloping so, all of a sudden."

"Galloping? Er . . . Well, this matter, as they say, must be chewed over."

Kuk rolled his leaden eyes, waved his walking stick and looked so stuffed with conceit that I could hardly restrain myself from laughing. He was a walking caricature. I looked at him, wondering how it was possible for such a character to have been preserved in the modern world, and, what's more, in such a great city.

But I no longer wished to be amused by the manager, and he soon began to make me feel nervous. I was continually looking round, staring at people, trying to spot the artist among them. I cursed the manager and sought wildly for an excuse to leave him.

"Eurveka!" Kuk cried out unexpectedly.

"Eureka!" I corrected him.

He may have blushed, for his eyes glistened. He turned away and said no more. He was very touchy, and any incident like "eurveka" upset him terribly. To distract from this awkward moment, I said: "Weren't you going to tell me something?"

"Yes, I was going to tell you something," he muttered almost inaudibly. "Tell me, why are you so angry with me?"

"When was I angry with you?" I asked in surprise.

"When you spoke of 'galloping.' Perhaps you thought I wanted to compromise you? If so, you are very unjust: God forbid!—my thoughts were far from it."

"What are you talking about?" I asked nervously.

"Perhaps you thought," said the manager, "that I was playing with you: in other words, nobody wants her, that is why she is not getting married!"

I laughed; it was impossible not to. This ape thought so highly of himself that he wanted to sympathize with me. "Perhaps you will take me for your wife?" I asked ironically. The manager hesitated: so even this ape would not have me for his wife. Even he. "Don't worry, Comrade Kuk," I said, "it's just a joke. I don't intend to get married."

The manager brightened up at once. Then I told him that I only wanted to be his mistress, and would like to give myself to him, because I was bored with life. I wanted him to come to my room and we would kill time together. I have always been opposed to the philistine family life with a geranium on the shelf. Why? One can do without it.

We came out upon a moonlit clearing. It was far from the main exit, and the city folk hardly ever came here. Only rarely would a couple come down a bypath and disappear behind the trees. An engine was clamoring loud and long at the station. The leaves were falling like soft rain.

I looked at Kuk: he was pressing close to me and was pale. Saliva (perhaps it was only my imagination) dribbled from his mouth. "You mean it?" he asked in a trembling voice and fell silent.

"Nothing but the truth!" I said.

Then he asked if I would let him sleep in my room. I asked him why—he did not answer. I said that I wanted to sleep in his room. Kuk sighed: that was out of the question, his mother was paying him visit. I asked him what we should do. The manager was silent. I had an idea and said: "What if we went into the bushes?" He shudderingly agreed. He pressed himself even more closely to me, and with his right hand caressed my left breast. Carefully I removed his hand. Then the manager stopped. "I have just thought," he said, "how much does an abortion cost these days?"

"Why do you want to know?" I asked.

Kuk hesitated again. Then I understood him and said "I won't ask anything from you for an abortion."

The manager brightened up once more. He looked at me gratefully, pressing himself still more closely against me. Then we moved quickly towards the bushes. The sky was so beautiful, but a stone lay at the bottom of my heart. I had completely forgotten Charhar, as if I were really only interested in Kuk --the manager with the face of an ape.

The violoncello still grieved over the park. The moon stood above a gigantic oak and continued indifferently on her heavenly way. I walked silently at the side of the manager, but I could not then find words to express the storm that boiled in my breast. Suddenly I stopped. "You know," I said, "I don't intend to have an abortion!"

"Why?" Kuk stopped too.

"It's quite simple: I want to give birth to a child."

The manager was nonplussed. I understood, and said that he would be well advised to think a little before going any further. He was not an eighteen-year-old youngster, and should know the facts of life. "You mean alimony?" He understood me immediately.

"Yes, I mean alimony."

Then Kuk whistled and said firmly that he refused to go on because his pocket would not stand it and that he would rather take on a prostitute. He had hardly spoken the last word when with all my might I struck him across the face. Kuk paled and stood with downcast eyes.

But I had already cooled down. "Why have I struck him?" I thought, feeling my heart wither away. The point is that, on the whole, I never considered anybody on earth guilty, and I have always regarded myself as an absolute wretch. Kuk was such a small, insignificant dot that I felt painfully sorry for him. Then, leaning on a tree I said almost inaudibly: "Forgive me, Comrade Kuk. Do what you like, but don't be angry with me!"

"It's nothing! It's nothing!" he said, "This will remain between us. I don't intend to discharge you from your position." I only heard that. That phrase cut through my breast like a knife; he had misunderstood me.

The manager had long ago disappeared behind the trees, but I still stood near the oak, on the deserted path, looking dully at the blue sky.

VI

It was winter before I succeeded in meeting Charhar. Then I saw him several times. But these meetings were cold—they only made me nervous. I even began to avoid him. But all this time I felt that I had left something unfinished and must needs finish it. The fact that this something must be completed made it as inevitable as death.

I wandered about with an empty heart, but considered this state to be merely temporary, a necessary and quite natural stage on the dark road of my restless life. In the morning I would go to the office and work there for eight hours; then I would take some work home and carry on for a few hours longer.

The winter was wet and dirty. Out on the streets the lamps were continually sunk in fog, and I had no desire to go outside.

At times Comrade Ulyana would visit me, but I rarely talked with her. Sometimes I would write letters to my mother, and then long-buried thoughts would again awaken within me: that spotlessly white cottage, the rooster on the vane and the dark, provincial gardens. But I never felt drawn home now —I already knew that there would be no going back for me.

I was roused by the spring, as was to be expected. This new spring was the beginning of my end. Early in March I felt alarmed again, and my winter dream suddenly vanished; once more I began to long for the mysterious Distance. But this longing was so intolerable that I wondered whether I was not ill. With this longing came impetuosity, joyous laughter, and freedom from care. Sometimes I would look at myself in the mirror. There I saw two warm, moist, dark cherries—they were my eyes.

Even Charhar was moved by the season. Once he sent me a letter asking me to visit the young woods on the outskirts of the city. "My beautiful Bianca," he wrote, "the day smells so fragrantly of spring, and I feel so drawn by Distance (that is what he wrote,

Distance), the geese have flown back from warmer climes, and we must see the sunset. Are you willing?"

Why not? How could I refuse? On the way I bought a chocolate bar, and licked my lips nervously

At times I worked as long as fifteen hours a day but I lived as I pleased, so they called me the Princess, in the office. I loved chocolates, blue sky, and the artist's lovely eyes.

I met Charhar, as arranged, near the square of "The Three Communards." I squeezed his hand tightly, and he responded. As I entered the coach Charhar accidentally touched my breast. This excited me so much that all the way I felt my nostrils dilating

As we drove out of the last city street, and the steppe unfurled its endlessness before us, I looked at Charhar and said "Why were you so cold towards me all this winter?"

"You must guess," he said, smiling, "all the sullen people in the city have felt like that this winter."

"All?" I asked, "The communists and the Soviet employees, all those perhaps who are unable to reconcile themselves to their surroundings?"

"Absolutely all!" he said with a smile.

"Then—that means that you, too, belong among the sullen people?"

I suddenly wondered whether Charhar was in the same difficult position as I, and was suffering the same little pains. This dawned upon me so suddenly that I laughed. I laughed either out of joy that I was not completely alone in my troubles, since they were shared by so great an artist, or else because I felt bitterness, since my idol had fallen from its base.

"And what do you mean, sullen people?" I asked

"What do you mean?"

"That phrase is as old as the world itself," he said, evading a reply.

"I don't remember ever having heard it."

I was lying, and Charhar noticed it. Then he bit his lower lip. He always did this when he was nervous. I made up my mind not to bother him, and we drove on in silence.

We got down from the coach about ten versts away from the city. We told the driver to wait, and went to the edge of the wood. The brief sun was just setting. A crystal silence reigned. The trees were still naked, but the early Spring was victoriously approaching from the south. Green grass was showing here and there, while birds were clamoring everywhere.

We walked on in silence for a time. Then we exchanged a few phrases (I don't remember them now). Suddenly Charhar stopped and said, "I want to leave you for about five minutes. You don't mind?"

"Not at all," I said quietly, supposing that he wanted . . . Well, in short, it was understood.

Charhar went, and I was left alone in the forest. Then I looked again at the sky. It was unusually clear and young. From the south a cloudlet was approaching but it soon melted away into space. I sighed deeply and thought of unknown worlds, of millions of solar systems. These thoughts seemed to weigh me down. I felt terribly small and insignificant. All my pains and joys seemed as ridiculous against the background of this grandiose cosmos as the sufferings of an insect seemed to me. I reflected that millions of people had had these thoughts for thousands of years, and that millions of others would go on doing so for thousands of years to come. Then the enchanted puzzle appeared so clear that it was as if I had sensed it with a new feeling I had not yet experienced.

Charhar left me alone for more than ten minutes, and this frightened me. He might have had an accident. Resolutely I set off in the direction he had taken. I pushed through a thicket whose branches continually clawed at my head. I walked for a long time (it seemed to me then), but there was no sign of Charhar. The forest was unusually quiet and hushed. The farther in I went the duskier it grew. Then it struck me that I might lose my way, and I was worried. I stopped and called out: "Hi!" An answering echo died down somewhere in the thicket. "Like the forest of life," I thought, and flung myself in another direction. Suddenly I emerged upon a glade and stopped as if rooted to the ground. I could not have done otherwise, for among the trees knelt Charhar, his face towards the evening sun, and he seemed to be praying. It astonished me so much that I could find no words, and waited for him in silence.

On a distant tree glowed a streak of the dying sun, its reflection falling on the southern edge of the dark forest. It was a beautiful moment for observation. I thought of India and of the sacred hymns of Ramayana. "Perhaps in Tagore's native land" I thought, "my chimerical Distance has been found."

Finally Charhar rose. He walked up to me quietly as though nothing had happened. His step, literally, hypnotized me, and I met him in silence.

"Come!" he said quietly.

His eyes were vague, he staggered as though intoxicated. I remember he sighed and took my hand. Then he took my other hand and pressed it to his heart. A feeling of joy seized me, for Charhar had come closer than ever before. I did not want to scare him away with frequent, unsuccessful questions, so I remained silent. But this time it was he who was the first to begin talking.

"Bianca," he said, "I think you understand my spiritual state, and will forgive me for making you wait so long for me."

"I understand you," I said.

Then he said that he felt almost like Moses coming down the mountain with his tablets. Then, for some reason, Charhar smiled as though he himself did not believe in what he said, or, perhaps, because he had spoken his last phrase about Moses ironically.

"I understand you," I repeated.

"It is impossible for you not to understand me. I have more than once thought that we are kindred souls."

"Kindred souls?" I asked, a little too quickly.

"Yes, kindred souls!" Charhar emphasized.

This last phrase struck me as if with a physical blow: he too believes that we are alike! I made no move to betray this to Charhar. I was now so afraid lest he should stop speaking freely: I knew him well enough by this time—and I realized that the least curiosity on my part would immediately cause a recoil, and he would again become remote.

"You know," he stopped suddenly, "there in the glade a great thought flashed in my brain, a thought whose existence I hardly suspected. Strange," he continued, "I seemed to be sitting in a cellar, and above me there was a club of . . . well, what's its name?"

"Of Soviet Employees."

"Why, yes, of Soviet Employees," he said, becoming nervous all of a sudden.

"Why are you worried?" I asked.

"Because," he cried out, and his voice seemed a childish soprano, "I cannot stand the self-confidence of our age. All these cells, commissars, communists —it is all such cheap demagogy . . . Such . . ."

Charhar could not find the right word, and stopped. Then he looked carefully into my eyes and said softly: "Can I trust you?"

"What is the matter with you?" I asked in astonishment.

"I trust you," he said, holding his head with both his hands. "Ah, Bianca, how can I make you understand me! Well, how? Well why do we have these communists, these cells, these professional unions and thousands of other organizations? Goodness, why? I gasp for breath. I have nothing against them—God forbid! Let them conquer the whole world. But what have I to do with it? Why must I look around me every minute, why must I listen to these meetings? My God, how I wish they would ignore my existence!"

Once more Charhar held his head in despair and fell silent. I looked at him. He was weeping. He was really weeping, I saw a few tears roll down his cheek. Then I felt an unbearable contempt for him and said sharply: "Mr. Charhar, what is the matter with you?"

He stood with his back to me, leaning on a tree. He remained thus for about two minutes. But when he turned I saw again the remote artist of old.

"Anything happens in life," he said finally in a completely different, cold tone.

I looked at him in surprise. Perhaps Charhar realized how far he had gone in his conversations with me, and had hastened to smooth out the tracks. This was the reason for the sorry melodrama. This thought seemed so real to me that next day I had quite forgotten this particular episode. "Well, no," I thought, "now you are in my hands—and I will force you to say what you have left unsaid."

We stood once more at the edge of the forest. The sun had already set. The forest was dark, and the gloomy road wound by. Far in the distance our carriage was standing on the road. We entered it quickly and returned to the city, Charhar silent all the way, and we parted in silence too. I remember pressing his hand, and holding it for a moment. He shuddered, but still I would not let go his hand. Then Charhar had to force it out. I laughed, but he did not react in any way. He simply turned and walked away from me at a quickened pace.

VII

A few days later I met Charhar again, but the meeting was not important—and so I will omit it. I parted from him when the young crescent moon was already high up in the sky. On Delacluse Street I met the grey-eyed journalist. She asked me to give her five roubles. I handed them over. She said she was going to see her mother who lived in the northern end of the city. She wanted to buy her a gift. Of course, I did not believe her, I knew she was on the way to her lover—who was, it appeared, secretly a rake. She seemed a little puzzled, but later she stopped me by a lighted show-case and asked in a whisper if I would go with her. She and her lover wanted to arrange a night of drinking and love. "Come, Bianca dear, we'll have some beer," she feebly attempted a rhyme, smiling. I replied that possibly I might have gone had I not been a virgin.

"What do you mean?" she asked in astonishment.

I repeated it and tried to leave. Then she seized my hand, guffawing loudly. "So you haven't yet . . ." and she added a vulgar expression. Then, pushing me to one side she asked breathlessly: "You're not lying when you say you haven't known a man?" I swore I was speaking the truth, and suddenly felt enveloped with a flame of desire. Then the grey-eyed journalist pressed my arm just above the elbow so painfully that I had to push her away. She told me that I was a beauty, that they would give a thousand roubles for my body, that such women live in Odessa and Moscow where there are many bourgeois men with money. In other words, I must go with her at once and I would discover a life that was beyond the dreams of this world.

She painted attractive pictures. But she looked at me with such wild eyes that I had to push her aside again.

"Aren't you coming with me?" she finally cried out in despair.

"No!"

I spoke firmly. Then she swung her arm as if to strike me on the face. But I caught her hand just in time and saved myself. I held her so strongly that she was forced down to her knees. I had not suspected that I possessed such strength. Suddenly the journalist started to weep. Then I kissed her hand (it smelled of cheap powder) and helped her into the street-car. She rode off and I went home.

I went home down the alleys at a leisurely pace. A slight fear made me tremble continually. At the Square of the Rebellion I stopped at a candy counter and bought a bar of chocolate.

An hour and a half later I arrived home and sat down at the table. I remember Comrade Ulyana came to my window and asked if I would like to go to the summer-house for a while. I did not feel like leaving my room, so I said, "Isn't it a little too cool outside?"

"What are you talking about?" asked Comrade Ulyana.

I did not know what to say. We went out to the summer-house. Seated on the bench, we began to talk. After half an hour of unimportant chatter, Comrade Ulyana suddenly asked me—"Do you believe in fate?"

"Well, how should I put it . . . Of course not."

"You know," she said, "theoretically, I don't believe in it myself. In fact I am not allowed to believe in it myself (she meant apparently her belonging to the Party), but in practice things turn out differently."

"Do you, by any chance, think," I said, "that the existence of idealistic theories is justified?"

Comrade Ulyana denied this with a flutter of her hands.

"What are you talking about! How could such a

thought occur to me!" she said, frightened. "I only think that in the world there are two outlooks which continually alternate. But if idealism leaves much to be desired, I think that materialism, too, is not without its weaknesses."

"In other words, your Party does not satisfy you?"

Comrade Ulyana again denied this with a flutter of her hands.

"Nothing of the kind! I only wish to clarify my outlook. You know," she continued, "I never used to think about these things before, but now they frighten me terribly."

"Nothing happens without a cause," I reasoned, "there must be some reason for your fear."

"That's it!" exclaimed Comrade Ulyana, promptly taking the hint. "You are right in saying that. You know, I feel some danger threatening. I am certain that some misfortune will soon happen to me."

The deduction was not very logical, but I did not point this out and merely tried to soothe her. But she clung to this thought, and nothing could calm her. "A misfortune—I am sure," Comrade Ulyana said, "I am never wrong. Once, at the front, I suddenly thought during the night that we would be surprised. I said so, but they would not believe me. One commissar even suggested that I ought to be turned out of the Party for such a prophecy. Yet it happened as I said: our staff was surrounded, and I was the only one to escape."

"Well, that's exceptional," I said.

Then Comrade Ulyana protested again, and I stopped arguing with her. I merely thought that, perhaps, Comrade Ulyana was right in her obstinacy, and I thought too, that she was one of those failures who come into this world only to suffer.

Suddenly, across the gardens there came flying to us a roar from the zoological gardens: it was a lion roaring behind bars. The roar was rather sad and desperate. Perhaps the beast was dreaming of the distant spaces of his native land, perhaps—of something else.

"There!" Comrade Ulyana said emphatically, "the lion is roaring! Sometimes human beings feel like roaring too." Then she sighed. Afterwards she told me a great deal about the civil war. She talked of those wild and frightful times when people walked naked and hungry, and were both giants and gods. She was so carried away that no poet could have equalled her description. I had brushed this fantastic period with only one wing of my youth, but Comrade Ulyana was quite mistaken in thinking I did not understand it. It was dear to my heart. I thought that then everyone partook of the mysterious Distance, but that time would never again return, as my sky-blue youth would never return again.

"Then even my mysterious Distance, must it be sought on some other highways?" I thought.

Next day I did not go to work. I awoke with a headache. While I was boiling my tea, someone knocked along the corridor. I opened the door. Comrade B. came in. His face was creased and pallid: obviously he had not slept all night. Up to this time I had never spoken to him (he was so stern and unsociable). But this time I ventured somewhat mechanically: "Good-day!"

He looked at me in astonishment and winked his

103

left eye. Then I, in my turn, looked at him with surprise. I noticed that he was drunk. To get rid of him I told him that Comrade Ulyana was waiting for him.

"Did you say Ulyana?" he asked and came up to my fire.

"Yes!"

Comrade B. took a cigarette case out of his pocket and surprised me with: "You know, you are . . . quite a girl!"

I looked at him severely and said he had better go to his room.

"Why there?" he muttered drunkenly.

"Comrade Ulyana is waiting for you there!" I said sharply.

Comrade B. stamped and said something indecent about his wife. I turned sharply and went into my room. For quite a while I thought of Comrade Ulyana's life, but how to help her I did not know. And yet, perhaps, it only seems to me now that I worried about Comrade Ulyana. Perhaps Comrade Ulyana, the grey-eyed journalist, and the manager —perhaps they had all been giving me a rest—and nothing else. For really, they were all, on the whole, episodic persons in my story, and could not interest me. I was simply deceiving myself.

But all this had to come to an end, and the end came.

VIII

So spring was coming and the nightingales returned. Sometimes I went to the theater, but more often I wandered about the city like a stray dog. I continued to be troubled by a slight terror. But I roamed about like a carefree peasant, and whistled. In those days I ate more chocolate than I had eaten in my whole life before.

The May Day celebrations were approaching. The day before I took a bath, washed, and perfumed my body. I did this as carefully as if I were preparing for my wedding night. I put on a gown with rose-colored ribbons and went to bed.

I awoke about eight o'clock and felt happier and more lighthearted than ever before. It was a fine spring morning. The orchestras were already playing out on the streets, and the cars were rushing into the country outside the city. I dressed quickly and hurried to the office. We were to gather there, and then go on to the hippodrome. The local committee had appointed me organizer, and I tied a red handkerchief around my arm. In the first corridor I met the manager. I greeted him, but he did not reply. Ever since our last conversation he had avoided me and seldom came up to my desk. Nevertheless, he treated me quite politely. This was not so much the result of his integrity, but because the local communist group thought well of me (I was a real social-worker in the office), and Kuk was terribly afraid of the communists and always trotted before them on his hind legs.

We marched in serried ranks to Lassale Square and from there to the hippodrome. All the streets were bursting with people. May Day, I thought, had already become our national holiday, for it was celebrated even by the bourgeoisie. I thought of Paris,

France, and of the international holiday there, and reflected that we had much in common with the French. I said this to a typist walking beside me. She answered unintelligently, for she was terribly limited. But the grey-eyed journalist heard our conversation and came up to me.

"Do you think it is possible to draw a parallel between us and France?" she asked.

"Yes!"

"In what way?" and she looked at me malevolently.

I told her. I said that the great French Revolution reminds us strongly of ours, that . . . etc.

"You talk like Cicero!" she said ironically.

"What has Cicero to do with this?" I asked.

"What?" and she became fidgety all of a sudden. "And what have you to do with politics . . . sticking your nose in it?"

"Even supposing I am mistaken," I said calmly, "still haven't I the right to think?"

The grey-eyed journalist looked at me in silence and stepped aside. At this moment our group halted: we had reached the hippodrome.

There was a sea of flowers on the immense field, and there was a rumble from about ten orchestras. On the principal square the pioneers and komsomols were doing physical exercises. From several platforms orators were delivering their speeches. Sirens roared, automobiles swarmed around. In half an hour large groups were crumbling into small groups, and in a while individuals were seen wandering about. Then temporary troupes set up temporary stages, and several miniature theaters sprang up in the field.

I left my group and went wandering. I simply had

to meet Charhar somewhere around here, for I could not imagine his not coming.

I remember I stopped at stall No. 4. I bought a bottle of kvas and drank it greedily. Then I went to the painters' screen. There, in five minutes, artists painted caricatures of the men of the Revolution. There I met Charhar. He was happy and gaily pressed my hand. "It is an unusually wonderful morning," he said. I pressed myself close to him and we left. We wandered about the hippodrome for about an hour and then set out for the steppe. I began to tease him a little.

"You know," I ventured, "today you are not walking with a girl, but with a married woman!"

"What do you mean by that?" he asked.

I laughed, and told him I was married. For some reason he reddened and, bowing gallantly, became interested: "May I ask who your husband is?"

"Manager Kuk," I said, "I think you know him."

"Yes, I know him. It seems . . . he is a wonderful man!"

I was certain he did not believe me and that he was joking. So I changed the subject, not attempting to correct him. We were walking in a sea of immortelles. To the right of us an immense radio tower soared up to the sky. I remember I suddenly thought that Charhar might have a slight fever.

"You seem a little tipsy today," I said.

"I am a little tipsy," and he smiled.

I asked him why so early. He said that for several days past he had been starting the day with vodka. He did not like vodka much, but he could not deny that the "vodka days" were less troublesome and much happier. "Did he really weep seriously then, in the forest?" I thought, and said: "Why is your outlook on life so hopeless?"

"What makes you think that?" and Charhar smiled.

Then he assured me that life was very gay. He laughed a good deal that day, and so did I. With carefree laughter and talk we wandered about until the evening. Finally, Charhar said: "Well, it's time we went home. . . . Would you care to come to my rooms?"

I agreed and we set out for his apartment. We wandered through the streets for about half an hour until we emerged on the Square of the Three Communards. We reached Charhar's rooms as it was already growing dark. Unexpectedly a gypsy-woman came up to us. I said that she could tell my fortune. Charhar became fidgety, and said it was vulgar to flaunt one's lack of culture thus.

"That's being a quibbler!" I said.

Then I told him that he, too, had fallen into mysticism at times, hinting at the incident in the forest. Charhar became nervous. But I stubbornly insisted. Then he advised me to step aside so that the Soviet Employees would not see me from the club window. Finally I understood, and told the gypsy I did not wish to have my fortune told that day. Descending the flight of steps I turned to Charhar: "Tell me, had the gypsy woman come up to us somewhere in a deserted place, would you have allowed me to have my fortune told?"

Charhar was silent, but I knew without his telling me what he would have done then, and an unpleasant feeling towards the artist was roused within me.

In his room we sat down on the bed. I took a book in my hands. So did Charhar. Thus, silently, we sat for a few moments. Then a dark cloud spread over the sky, and it became almost quite dark in the room. The May Day orchestras were dying away somewhere. The city was growing calm. Drops rattled on the window and a heavy rain followed. A light wind swirled into the room, bringing in with it the smell of field flowers.

Although Charhar had spoiled my mood, I was still brimming with the impressions of the day, and that is why, when he placed his hand on my lap, I looked into his face with gratitude: in his eyes there was a gentle brilliance which reminded me of our first meeting. His eyes lured me again with their vagueness. The longer I looked at them the more the artist's body excited me. At last he took me by the hand and said: "Bianca, will you tell me today what you told me once before?"

"What was that?" I asked, startled.

Charhar hesitated and was silent. Then, resolutely, I walked to the light and put it out. Then I sat down again on the bed.

"Are you thinking of the gypsy woman?" I asked, consciously postponing the decisive moment.

Charhar was silent, stroking my hands. Then he kissed my fingers.

"Well, what were you thinking of?" I asked again.

"I meant . . ." he hesitated, and added firmly, "Didn't you once tell me you loved me?"

"Yes, I did."

He paused once more. Then, incoherently, he began to assure me that he, too, loved me, that . . . etc.

But—just a moment! He did not mean those words at all. It was only now that he felt how much he loved me. I remembered my little joke about my marriage to Kuk, and asked if his plight did not resemble that of Onegin. When Tatiana was free, he thrust her away from him. When she was married. . . . Well, it is quite clear: history repeats itself. Then Charhar began to swear that nothing of the kind had happened, and that these were my own inventions.

I became nervous. Could it really be the famous artist who was speaking? Just then a horrid thought flashed through my mind. Did he really believe I had married Kuk? Now I could see why he came to love me so suddenly! Alimony again! I began to sound him carefully.

"All right," I said, "suppose you love me and suppose I have deceived you?"

"How do you mean?" Charhar did not understand me.

"Well," I said calmly, "I had not even thought of getting married. It was simply a joke."

He drew away from me abruptly and became restless: as if to say, why such jokes? Besides, who gave me the right to tease him? (That is what he said —"who gave me the right"). Then I rose in a trice and switched on the light. I faced Charhar and said sharply: "What do you mean—who 'gave me the right'? What does this tone mean?"

He sat quiet and pale. It struck me that I was exaggerating, that perhaps I had not understood him (he certainly did not like to jest at serious moments), that I was making a fuss about nothing: Charhar had not even thought of offending me. I drew near to

110

him and put my arms around his neck. "My darling,"
I said, "don't be angry! Really, I offended you against
my will."

He looked into my eyes with a long and attentive
look. During these moments my breath was literally
blocked, and I needed air—was I so much disturbed?
In a single moment a million thoughts darted
through my head. They flashed like lightning one
after another.

"All right, I won't be angry with you," said the
artist. "But you must tell me: are you married or
not?"

Then a thought flashed within me and I said: "Yes,
I am, my darling, I am!"

Firmly he took me by the hand and placed me on
the bed. "Alimony," I thought faintly, and felt weak
in my whole body. Charhar caressed me. A fresh
wind rushed into the room, and once more came the
smell of field flowers. The heavy spring rain subsided, and the dark night peered through the window.
Charhar switched out the light. Carefully he made
me undress on the bed. He was on the point of
possessing me when I felt my strength return. I
jumped out of bed and once more put on the light.
I went up to Charhar. He gazed at me in astonishment. I looked at him calmly, spat in his face, and
went to the door in silence.

IX

Thus ended my affair with the artist. Thus,
ignobly, ended this holy (that is what he had said
—'holy simplicity'), and devoted love. How can I

write of the torment which possessed my romantic soul? Today I look on life quite realistically. Now I can even laugh at myself sometimes. But then the sentimental Distance glimmered in my eyes, and when I saw that even Charhar, my last hope, was unable to escape from the universal brothel, I became desperate.

Several days passed after that last meeting with Charhar, but it seemed to me as long ago and far away as that dim corner of my dead youth, as distant as those aromatic golden roosters I dreamed of, like the caramel suckers at the fair which, among the 'heart's case,' camphor, and mint, had cock-a-doodled through my childhood.

The evening of May Day had certainly thrown aside forever all my hopes and expectations, and I was brought up suddenly before the emptiness of the commonplace office days.

How I hated the artist then! My God, how I hated him! Not until then did I realize that the spotlessly white cottage, the golden rooster on the vane, and the dark provincial gardens—all had been forsworn for his sake. At first, as might have been expected, I wanted to be revenged for my broken hopes. I wanted to humiliate Charhar and show him what he deserved. But after a while even this desire cooled down within me and I simply stopped thinking of him—so small and insignificant did he become in my eyes.

But the longing for Distance still clung to me. Indeed it flamed up wilder than ever. This was its last flicker.

None of the Soviet Employees took upon themselves as much work as I did in those days. Like a drunkard I gorged myself with it. I wanted to drown my unhappiness in it. But cynicism was gnawing at me. The work seemed a trivial and altogether unnecessary chore carried out for trivial and insignificant people who lived like bulls and cows, and whose interests were limited by the geranium on the table; I took an active part in the womens' organizations, in meetings of delegates, and in the editing of the local wall-newspaper, but I always thought that our paper was not quite accidentally called "stin-gas."[5] It was exactly what it expressed—gas, smoke. Wet straw was burning and people sat around this illusory bonfire and thought that 'there is no smoke without a fire.'

Once, as I was leaving the office, I met the grey-eyed journalist in the doorway. She looked at me rather rudely, took me by the arm, and went along with me. When we reached the theatrical gardens, she said: "Well, are you still thinking of Paris?"

"Which Paris?" I asked.

"My God," she said, "why hide it from me? I am talking of the Paris of—the Great French Revolution."

"I refuse to understand you!" I returned coldly.

Then the grey-eyed journalist assured me that that Paris would never return, never. She said that she quite saw through me. But she advised me not to worry, for I was not at all what I thought I was.

"You know," she suddenly said, "there are many unnoticed people. . . . Well . . . commissars, for

---

[5] Abbreviation of "stinna hazeta"—the wall newspaper.

example; but they live just like others. And just because of that they are regarded as heroes. And what are you? Well, tell me—what are you?"

I shrugged and kept silent, for I really did not understand what she wanted of me. Then the journalist patted me on the back and burst out laughing.

"Listen," she said, "you had better follow my footsteps before it's too late."

Then she left me and I went home.

I did not eat lunch that day. An idea was boring its way incisively into my head, and I stubbornly kept it at bay. Thus several hours passed.

In the corridor Comrade Ulyana was stirring the fire in the samovar with her shoe. It was several days after she had visited me, and it occurred to me that I was treating her more coldly than I intended. Then I thought of her broken nose, and it stopped before me in a kind of stubborn blot. I thought, too, of Comrade B. and of his dishevelled head, and could certainly not imagine him playing the part of a young man in love.

Suddenly, a bird lighted near my window and chirped out its song. It seemed so dreamlike on the background of the dark-blue sky that it reminded me of a child's tale about happiness: "Once upon a time there lived an old couple, and a bird came to them . . ." The Jew's children were yelling in the yard, and I thought of the old Jew still philosophizing over the Talmud, just as other old Jews philosophized a thousand years ago.

It grew quite dark in my room, and I thought of the mysterious "golem," the snatching devil, and the Judgment Day of the Jewish colony.

The evening was drawing to a close. Comrade Ulyana was still stirring the fire in the samovar. A siren clamored obstinately somewhere. And then I suddenly felt that I was no longer worthy to try to escape myself.

"So the journalist suggests that I had better follow her footsteps before it is too late?" I said, "What does she mean—before it is too late? My God, what is happening to me! Aha! Now I even say 'My God!'" I thought.

Just then, suddenly, everything became clear to me. And indeed, had I not been struggling with a god all this time? I wanted to clutch the semi-abstract Distance with my own strength. But without 'Him' (I wrote 'Him', for he was then truly my inevitable fate) it was impossible to succeed. I wanted to clutch this Distance without 'Him', and he could not forgive me for this.

"Yes," I thought, "this is the punishment for my impudence."

I got out of bed. I had never yet believed in God, and that is why I turned towards Him with that strength of new feeling felt by fanatics when they turn to Heaven. I felt I had to go down on my knees before the picture of a "savior."

Quietly I went to the door and into the corridor. In Comrade Ulyana's storeroom I had once seen an old ikon: Comrade B. had apparently thrown it there. I decided to take it and put it in my room. But how? Comrade Ulyana always had her storeroom closed and I had to get the key. But immediately I remembered that she kept her iron in the storeroom. Then I went to Comrade Ulyana to ask for the iron. I knocked. She came out with a cloth tied around her head.

"What is the matter with you?" I asked.

She reddened and looked at me with her sad eyes. She said she had been careless and had scalded herself with water from the samovar, but it would soon be better. Naturally, I did not believe her, for the blue marks under her eyes told a different story. It was Comrade B.'s affair: he had very likely beaten her the night before.

Comrade Ulyana sighed heavily and said: Poor Comrade B."

We stood facing each other in silence in the semi-darkness of the corridor, for about half a minute. Then I heard the rats rustling in the storeroom and said: "Will you lend me your iron?"

Comrade Ulyana bestirred herself and hurried into the room. I thought she would bring me the key, but she brought the iron; it was on the stove. And so, I did not get the key that time. However, I got it later, after sundown.

The ikon, which I seized stealthily and with fear, was an old board, and the face of the "savior" had an unusually attractive outline, though it was only suggested. I felt better at once. I brought him into the room, tied a small string to him (to it, to the ikon) and hung it in the corner. Then I hurried into town and bought a votive lamp and a bottle of oil from a shopkeeper near the market place.

I went home and lighted the votive lamp before the "savior." I did not switch on the light, consequently the room was in a semi mystical dimness. To one side, in the storeroom, the rats were still bustling about.

Then I went down on my knees, crossed my hands on my breast, and, in silence, looked fervently at the picture of the "savior." I was praying. I prayed as fervently as I prayed in my childhood. Time and again I sighed heavily, and then imagined I was standing in the catacombs of the early Christians, carrying a heavy cross. There passed before me the fanatics of the Middle Ages, the Great Inquisition, and the sombre monasteries of my fatherland. Human suffering and man's way of the cross towards the universal Golgotha—all this appeared to me so clearly!

I looked at the picture of the "savior," but I thought of the dark night of our reality, lost in the mysterious cosmos, of the people of my fatherland who had been crushed by Fate, and I had an intense longing that this legend of a fantastic good angel might be transformed into a reality, and I rejoiced at everything pure that still remained within me.

"Little god! My dear, precious little god!" I murmured, looking attentively at the picture of the "savior."

Quiet, childish tears were rolling down my cheeks, and I firmly believed that some miracle would suddenly and unexpectedly happen. I knelt for several hours on end, but did not feel tired.

Darkness had been spread over the city for quite a while. The clock on the tower had struck two. Fresh air was continually rushing into my room, swaying the fiery tongue on the votive lamp. The rats still bustled in the storeroom. "Little god! My dear, precious little god!" I prayed fervently as I did when a child, when mother and I would leave our immaculate white cottage, and cross the provincial gardens on our way to church to welcome the glorious "resurrection of Christ."

I knelt all night long and did not rise until it grew quite light.

From that time on I lit the votive lamp daily, and daily I knelt before the picture of the "savior." At times I prayed for Comrade Ulyana, for the grey-eyed journalist, and even for Kuk. Charhar I never mentioned, not because I felt any malice towards him, but simply because he had somehow flown out of my head. He existed for me no longer; his place in my heart was filled by the picture of the "savior."

The spring passed, and the warm summer returned. I worked at the office as accurately as before; the communists, indeed, considered me an exemplary worker. Only I could not laugh any more or eat chocolate with as much enjoyment.

Once I came back from work terribly tired, and went to bed early. During the night I heard someone knock. I switched on the light and was about to go to the door and open it, when a knock thundered on the door. I think I was never afraid of anything. This time I simply grew angry. The impudence astonished me. It was so late in the night—and imagine somebody knocking so loudly at the door of a solitary young woman! I put out the light and went back to bed again. Somebody knocked at my door for about half an hour longer, but I paid no attention, drowsing away into sleep. A blot of moonlight fell on the back of my bed, and I thought of my youth and of my neighbor, the driver. He would beat his wife as stubbornly as this stranger, who stood behind the door, beat at its panels.

Finally I fell asleep. And I had a fantastic dream. I was on the point of a journey, or was expecting something to happen. There was to be a carnival the next day and a mandolin festival. Next day, near the beacon of the steppe, under the evening sky, there was the Decameron. Then my land, looking like an idealized Nice. Suddenly Don Quixote produced for public disputation a master's dissertation on the subject of "The Soul of Matter." Maestro Danton smiled.

"O Maestro!" cried out Don Quixote, "Even in my language *kalamar* sounds too prosaic, for it is associated with *palamar*.[6] But behold! I take this word and, like a Hindu fakir, enchant your dull ear with it. Then your manly voice will sound in the memoirs of your age like a tiger in the jungle. Take a pen, fill your *kalamar* and write."

Then Maestro Danton wrote. And his ancient kalamar, out of which daggers have been formed for the past two hundred years, was enchanted with such an insignificant detail as a reminiscence, as when he first took a pen in his fingers and with anxiety formed the first letter. It was "M." Mind? Magnanimity? Mutiny?—he did not know, but he wondered whether it was not Maria.

"I conjure you like a Hindu fakir!" cried out Don Quixote. "I want to grasp your soul, O Matter. Are you really like a tank, and will the power of my artistic intuition find a way into your somber soul?"

Maestro Danton smiled and made a royally ob-

---

[6] *kalamar*—an inkwell; *palamar*—a sexton.

scene gesture. Don Quixote fell silent. A barker roared out, thundered, shouted. A gypsy jumped up, darted in front of the public, and disappeared behind the shooting gallery. . . .

. . . .

"Phew, the devil! What a jumble!" I cried out and started from my sleep.

A dead night peered at me through the window. Apparently I had not slept long, for somebody was still knocking at my door. "Are you knocking? Well, knock!" I thought, and drowsed again into sleep. Then I dreamt another dream.

On the outskirts of a village, where, to the right, there was an empty field and an ancient Cossack church, there stood a hut on a chicken's legs. And the hut was like a fairy tale, like a Pushkin nurse maid, like Hoffmann, like the sprites of Wilde, like the Thousand and One Nights. Bats were noiselessly flying into the night. The screech-owl hooted frightfully, "Oo-hoo!"

Inside the hut there was myself, a speculator, a provocateur, a murderer, and my sister—a prostitute. My sister had just come back from a secret inn and was sitting by the stove, near a Siberian cat. The cat was eternally purring.

"But how will I wash my hands?" I was thinking with anguish, "when they are covered with human blood? To whom will I tell my suffering—I, a speculator, a provocateur, a murderer? Yesterday, on the highway hidden by the almond hillocks that separate the Charles XII tract, I murdered a woman with a child. Three days ago I set the whole country guessing."

"Bianca," my sister turned to me suddenly, in her eyes ineffable sorrow, "what an anguish is mine!"

Then I turned and saw bright lances on the pristine steppe, above the wind-seared feather-grass. A horse was moving, and the steppe looked like a flaming mirage. A thousand and one nights, a forgotten country, honeyed landscapes, the exotic touch of long-horned oxen.

"Is this what Charhar will take to place on the altar of universal art?" I thought.

Then my sister again interrupted me with affliction in her voice: "Bianca, do you hear?"

"Hear what?" I cried out, "You wretch. Quiet, you jade!"

My sister buried her face in the wool of the Siberian cat and wept softly.

"Sister!" I continued, "do you know who will be the caesar of the future empire—the universal millionaire or the universal bureaucrat?"

And my sister spoke through tears: "How queer you are, Bianca, does this thought terrify you too?"

Then the hut on chicken's legs began to sway. I felt I was moving. I wanted to fall asleep so badly. My sister stroked my head. The room was a coffin —there was such dead silence in it, and suddenly my eyes paused: they found a spot.

"*Morituri te salutant!*" I cried out like the Roman gladiators who passed by their emperor on the way to battle.

But this was only a presentiment. There was silence around me, and only a cricket, like the official mourner over a dead body, chirped its recitative. Then I went up to the window and saw on the dark-blue background of the illimitable sky, above the Cossack church which stood solitary on the edge of the village in the windy expanse a gigantic black silhouette. It was such a senseless apparition that I drew back from the window in spite of myself. But in vain; for the wild she-cat of horror had already touched me with her fawning paw. Again she touched me, so softly, and so strongly. My heart dropped and crumbled apart with an almost inaudible and yet frightful bell-sound. I strained my thoughts to remember where I had seen that gigantic silhouette in a kepi.[r]

"O distant one!" I suddenly cried out again and as if mad leaped out of the hut that stood on a chicken's legs.

And again the lifeless, empty field, and the nocturnal, dark-blue sky unfurled themselves before me. "Where has it fallen?" I thought, "Where is this creation of genius in a kepi?"

Than I saw that where it fell there glimmered three mounds. And in those mounds lay three knights in medieval head-dresses. And the first said: "Morituri te salutant!"

. . . .

Again I awoke. There were cold drops of perspiration on my forehead. An urban dawn was already peeping through my window. I rose and put on my

<hr />

[r] Lenin.

slippers. I was filled with a strange presentiment. Something drew me to the door. In despair I opened it, and there at my feet, I saw the bleeding corpse of Comrade Ulyana, her head split in two. But strangely I did not even cry out. I only thought that, apparently, Comrade B. had killed her. "Poor Comrade B." I thought of her warm phrase.

Then I closed the door and went up to the ikon (a lamp was glowing in front of it). At first I looked at the picture of the "savior" in astonishment, and then said sternly: "Well, little god! Why did you not open the door when your handmaid Ulyana was knocking at it? Well?"

The room was in semi-darkness which was gradually being invaded by an urban dawn. The ikon lamp was still flickering and making fantastic shadows on the picture of the "savior." It was still and solemn in the room.

But I was beside myself with rage. A wild anger drilled my brain, and a dreadful insult lay on my heart. The face of the "savior" was none other than that of the dead Charhar. I drew back from the ikon and went up to the window. I literally swallowed air, for I felt that I would choke any minute. Then I approached the "savior" and, with no less delight than when I did so to Charhar, I spat on his beautiful face. Then I took a kitchen knife from the table and cut the picture into bits. I extinguished the ikon lamp and threw it out through the window.

Dawn was coming up. I went into the corridor, stepped over the bloody corpse of Comrade Ulyana, and went out into the streets. In the corridor, around the cloven head, there was naturally a great deal of blood, and my skirt was spattered with it.

I walked slowly. I went out along the road leading to a dull provincial district. Then I turned sharply and walked to Kuk's rooms. A train of wagons filled with refuse drove past me, and the street was suddenly full of the heavy stench of garbage. But I did not turn aside, on the contrary—I drew greedily through my nose the heavy smell of the city's corruption.

Probably there was a light blue sky above me, but I did not notice it. I emerged upon a new road where everything was so simple and clear, where people lived and died like true epicureans. This road had never been enigmatic to me, and I knew how many rebellious people had walked down it. This emboldened me. I came upon the Square of the Three Communards and turned into a crooked alley.

X

At this point I would be forced to end my pallid tale, were it not for a little detail which should finally point the way to my last god.

I reached Kuk's rooms to find him still in bed. I knocked. He appeared in his underwear and begged my pardon. I told him I had no objection to it. As usual, he did not understand me. I explained everything to him, saying that I was willing to give myself to him, but on one condition: that he immediately get me a messenger. At first Kuk did not believe me —he was afraid I might deceive him again. But the early hour and my pale face convinced him that I was not joking. He bestirred himself.

Then I went into his room and sat down at the table. On the envelope I wrote: "To the artist, Charhar," and in the letter asked Charhar to come quickly to Kuk's rooms (I gave the address), otherwise I would immediately give myself to the manager. I wrote that I was not yet married and never intended to marry. But this morning I wanted to donate my innocence. If he came on time—I would give it to him, if not—the manager with the apelike face would take it.

I wrote very incoherently, but none the less Charhar could not fail to understand me. Then I gave the letter to the messenger.

When the messenger had hurried out, I seated myself beside Kuk and embraced him. He smelled unpleasantly of sweat, and I thought: "refuse wagons." Then I let him take me.

I had not risen from the bed when someone knocked at the door. I knew who was there. I took the sheet and carried it out of the room.

Charhar was pale. I pointed to the blood (for a moment the thought of Comrade Ulyana's cloven head flashed into my mind) and smiled as I said: "Here is the remains of my innocence—take it, if you wish."

Charhar was silent. I turned sharply and went to my office.

———

Translated by C. H. Andrusyshyn.

THE INSPECTOR-GENERAL

In the lodging of Valentine Brodsky, the provincial newspaper reporter, preparations had been under way since morning for the visit of a very special guest. In fact, "the Comrade from the Center" should have lunched with the editor, but the editor, Ivan Sirko, was not in a position to receive him. To begin with, Sirko himself lived in a room much too small for him and his wife, and secondly, his Spartan quarters could under no circumstances serve as the setting for a banquet in honor of the "Comrade from the Center."

The reporter's wife, Lesya, had dashed across to the neighbors for advice as soon as she got up.

She wanted to receive the guest with appropriate honor; she even thought of buying some wine, horil-ka, and a couple of cans of food, but unfortunately she had no suitable china on which to serve it all, and, even more important, no money with which to buy it.

It was true that Sirko would gladly have helped her out with a few roubles from his own pocket, but Valentine was firmly opposed to the idea that his wife should prepare the luncheon with the editor's money and even opposed the borrowing of money for it from the editor. Brodsky was not only an exemplary host, but, in his own way, a truly ambitious man.

In the end Lesya managed to get hold of some money. But when she came back to pick up her shopping basket and co-op book, Valentine met her with a frown. He spoke with decision: "I am just going out. You shouldn't stay out so long, Lesya. Don't you realize that the inspector is probably already waiting in the editor's office?"

"Please wait a moment, Valentine," said Lesya, "I can't leave the children alone. Let me go to the co-op first."

Four-year-old Nelichka began to cry and two-year-old Murzyk whined a little too. The children realized immediately that their mother was going out again. "So you see, Valya? How can I leave them?"

Brodsky was annoyed because "it was so tactless to put him in such a ridiculous situation." He knew very well that his wife didn't want to leave the children alone, but she ought to realize that the inspector's visit was a very unusual event for him, and that he could not possibly stay at home when the "Comrade from the Center" might be sitting in the editor's office. A neighbor could be asked to look after the children. . . . And then what was this? What silly bourgeois prejudices: was this the way the workers-and-peasants children should be brought up? So Valentine advised his wife to lock the children up and so end the discussion. Let them cry; they would cry for a little while and then stop.

Although the reporter's wife was not convinced, she did not continue the argument. She let her husband go, and then asked a neighbor to look after the children while she went to the co-op.

By ten o'clock in the morning, the primus was hissing on the Brodsky's table, a luncheon was all ready at eleven. Finally, even the table could be forgotten: the bottle of horilka,[1] the bottle of Chateau d'Yquem, the can of sardines, the potatoes—they were all there on the table, waiting to be consumed. The guest could enter.

Guests, however, are very capricious. Having promised to come at one, let us say, they do not appear at one, and so everyone has to wait until four. But, unfortunately, they don't turn up at four, and at seven o'clock are still being expected. When the clock strikes half past seven, it is finally made known that the awaited guest will not come at all.

So it was with the "Comrade from the Center." In the evening Valentine came hurrying back to say that the inspector sent his regrets, but he could not possibly come to the Brodskys' that day . . . or rather he could not appear because the inspector and he (Brodsky) had already had a few drinks and something to eat at the tavern.

"Does this mean that he will come to lunch tomorrow?" asked Lesya.

"Tomorrow," faltered Valentine, slightly confused, "well, yes and no. You see, Lesichka, it's Sunday tomorrow and that means . . ."

"What?"

In sudden enthusiasm, the reporter rubbed his hands and with great zest began to inform his wife of the plans and prospects for the morrow. Accord-

---

[1] Ukrainian corn brandy.

ing to this plan, the next morning they, (that is, Lesya, himself, the editor, and the inspector), having taken all the food and drink previously prepared by Lesya, were to go by boat to Berestechko. There, they would hold a little picnic. They would return on the Kherson steamer in the evening. The trip (Valentine gave her his communist word of honor) promised many delightful experiences, provided the children were somehow taken care of.

The reporter felt somewhat guilty standing there in front of his wife. (After all, wasn't it possible to let her know about it earlier? Why did he keep her waiting around the primus?) He was also afraid that she might be offended by his behavior and scorn the idea of a picnic especially since he was so keen on it and he pressed her to accept it. However, his fears were not in the least justified, for, as soon as he stopped talking, Lesya embraced him and consented to go to Berestechko. What is more, without further thought she solved the problem of the children.

"On Monday," she said, "the laundry woman is coming to us. I'll ask her to come on Sunday—and so we'll be able to leave the children with her."

"That's excellent," said Valentine, a little surprised (he did not expect such ready agreement) and after playing for a while with the children, he went to bed. The luncheon at the time, it must be assumed, had been followed by a few beers, and therefore in a short time the reporter was peacefully asleep and blissfully snoring.

Lesya put the children to bed and went to see the laundry woman, who, fortunately, agreed to come on Sunday. Returning home, Lesya sat near the window and combed her hair. Any other night, especially after such a hectic day, she would have gone to bed at once, but now she could not even think of sleeping. It wasn't true that she had found it easy to agree to join the outing to Berestechko; that she was not offended by the tactlessness of her husband and their guest. The truth was, that, above all, the inspector's visit had excited her and the possibility of meeting him on an out-of-town picnic had thrilled her even more. What is more, she was thrilled as if with a forbidden joy. That is why she did not explain her feelings to her husband. She didn't intend to, either. Strangely enough, the news of the morrow's picnic had also stirred in her a feeling of gratitude to her Valentine.

And although nothing unusual had occurred, Lesya propped her elbows on the window sill and fell into a reverie, as wild as that of some exalted heroine of the romances she used to read long ago. Lesya even remembered Madame Bovary, and the thought of that woman evoked in her a tender and trembling feeling of anticipation.

The moon peeped suddenly from the eastern horizon and now it hung above the neighbor's shed. The little provincial town on the Dnieper grew quiet. One could hear neither the clatter of heavy carts nor the drone of trucks. The voices of the people bustling about on the market square died down too. The last steamer going south had hooted by long ago.

Lesya had been living for several years in this little provincial town. She had come here with Valentine from Kharkiv, where she had lived for only a year. She did not want to leave Kharkiv, but she had had to, since her husband was transferred to the province and she had loved him so very much, she could not let him go alone. She had come here in the settled conviction that she would return to Kharkiv soon. Had not Valentine himself promised to arrange that? Having come here, that is, she began to wait. Later, when it became clear that a farewell had to be said to Kharkiv, for a while at least, if not for good, Lesya did not wait any longer, all the more since Valentine had promised that even here, on this godforsaken bank of the Dnieper they would find "a full life." Later it grew clear that history was repeating itself, and that like the heroines in some of the novels, Lesya was doomed to a hopelessly monotonous existence, instead of living "a full life" or being in Kharkiv. It was then that Lesya gave herself up to contemplation.

Lesya was one of those ordinary female dreamers so numerous in the Ukraine. There is not much new one can say about them. The plot of this story is not very complex or unusual either. The visit of the inspector excited her so much not because the inspector, let us suppose, was a former lover of hers, but only because he came from Kharkiv—a city of which she had dreamed so often and which attracted her even more now that she had been away from it for so long. Like all provincial girls, Lesya was greatly impressed by Kharkiv. The buses, streetcars, opera, theaters, six-story buildings, the traffic in the streets —all this she still vividly remembered. Especially now, since it had receded into the past, all this city life assumed an unusual attractiveness. Like all the romantic young people of our republic, Lesya considered life in Kharkiv to be something almost fabulous. No wonder, therefore, she was so stirred by the arrival of somebody from that city. Since she regarded all the inhabitants of Kharkiv as definitely superior, she was anxious to hear whatever the inspector had to utter. And finally (this without doubt, subconsciously), couldn't she, a disappointed and frustrated woman, expect from the inspector something that might change her whole life?

Lesya looked at Valentine. He was lying with his arms spread out and his legs sticking out under the sheet. She looked at his feet, and after noticing how dirty they were, with long black toenails, she turned away. Yes, she thought, how can I expect anything outstanding from you, Valentine, if you don't even wash your feet?

Lesya remembered once more the sweet promises which Valentine had given her years ago, when they were leaving Kharkiv. She compared them with the reality in this small provincial town. Did not Valentine promise to help her to join the party? Didn't he assure her that she would never be aloof from the work in the little community? Didn't he speak of their family life as assuming a "New Meaning"? However, it turned out that instead of work in the community she had taken on the duties of a mother and a housewife. Instead of the family life with a "New Meaning" she had to endure constant small quarrels and be reduced to household slavery. Not being able to afford a servant (and her husband objected on principle to the idea of having a servant) she was confined to her home and children for the greater part of her dreary life here, with no time even to go to the movies. "Oh, Valya, my Valya," she ached with disappointment.

She loved her Valentine, but at the same time she saw how utterly helpless and really unhappy he was. This, at times, made her feel that he was an obstacle in her way. The spirit of restlessness still so much alive in her, was completely extinguished in her husband. At a time when she was still capable of bringing up and educating children, he was only capable of begetting them. Belonging to the young generation of the post-revolutionary period, Lesya could not become an ordinary tame city dweller, nor a person whose love for a man is quite uncritical. She was critical of her love for Valentine and it was because of that, that for the last year and a half she had come to regard it almost as a misfortune, or at any rate as voluntary slavery.

Nelichka woke up and started to cry. Lesya approached the cot. "Don't cry, my darling," she said softly and took the little girl in her arms. In a few minutes the child was asleep again. The moon shone on her auburn hair and Lesya imagined that her child's lovely curls were like the waves of inspired days. She took off her dress and stood there clad only in a shirt. Her cheeks flamed as she felt them with her palms. Something stirred in her almost girlish breasts and she felt as if she was going out to her first dance. The wind rose and stirred the silent streets. Valentine woke up. Seeing his wife was still awake, he said, "Aren't you asleep yet, Lesichka?"

"As you see, I have a headache."

"Do you perhaps feel like . . . ?" yawned Valentine stretching his arms towards his wife. "Perhaps?"

133

"No, please Valya, I am too tired tonight," Lesya said quickly. But the reporter had already seized her and was kneading her in his arms.

II

After a stormy night the wind dropped in the morning and only a light breeze remained. It played with the washing hung up on the line across the courtyard. Lesya was awake and looking through the window. The cocks were crowing and on the stable roof the neighbor's pigeons raced and cooed happily. Brodsky drank his tea and dashed off to the editor's where the inspector was spending the night. By the time he came back Lesya was giving instructions to the washerwoman. All they had to do now was to pick up their picnic basket and go to meet the steamer which was due to leave in half an hour. This they did.

On the jetty they met Sirko and the inspector. Valentine introduced his wife to the visitor from Kharkiv. "Topchenko," said the inspector, pressing Lesya's hand.

He was tall with a grey face and ugly eyes. But perhaps because Brodsky and Sirko were both small men, or because they lacked the confident manner of Topchenko, her husband and the editor appeared to Lesya as ridiculously tiny and helpless.

Coming up toward the harbor the inspector, as if inadvertently, put his hand on Valentine's shoulder, and having thus separated him from his wife, took Lesya by the arm. Brodsky was a jealous man and although he obviously didn't like the inspector's maneuver he didn't say anything and only smiled at the inspector, trying to tell him another absurd anecdote.

Lesya soon realized that her husband was making a fool of himself. He tried to appear funny and witty and sophisticated, but his weak, dark and weedy figure, his trivial jokes and his great desire to show off, made it all the more unmistakable that he was an out-and-out provincial and that he simply could not be compared with Topchenko. Sirko cut a better figure. Always silent and pensive, he was now more taciturn than ever, looking with his gray eyes at his feet. Only on those rare occasions when the inspector asked him a question would he suddenly quiver and show at once that he was very uneasy in the inspector's company.

"Is it possible that you like this wretched little town of yours?" asked Topchenko, addressing Lesya.

"We certainly don't," Brodsky quickly replied, waving his hands and slapping the inspector on the arm. "Que voulez-vous? What else can we do? You lucky people occupy the capital, and all we can do is to go there on a visit."

Topchenko looked contemptuously at Valentine and said: "Excuse me, I am not asking you. I was addressing your wife."

"Lesya?" fluttered Brodsky, "well, sure, Lesichka, why are you silent? Tell Comrade Topchenko what you think of our little town."

"Comrade Lesya must keep silent," said Topchenko ironically, "since you don't let her speak."

"I? Really? What an idea! Lesya, go on, tell him."

Valentine was confused and blushing, he thought

that perhaps the inspector realized that he was jealous of his wife.

"Yes," said Lesya at last, "I am terribly bored with this provincial place. You guessed right."

She kept her composure and betrayed her feelings neither to Topchenko nor to Valentine, but her anger at Valentine's behavior lasted for a good hour. When they reached the pier, Topchenko, without abandoning Lesya's arm, said to Sirko and Valentine, "Go ahead, and get on the boat, and we will join the line to buy tickets."

"What are you talking about?" exclaimed Brodsky, rushing toward the ticket office, "You are our guest. I'll buy the tickets."

"Well, if you insist," agreed the inspector without much argument, and having shaken off the editor he took Lesya into the waiting-room.

The boat was about to leave. Its siren was sounding for the second time and people were crowding the gangway. The passengers were a motley crowd. Among them were taciturn peasants, noisy market women who, after selling their fruits and vegetables were returning to their villages, workers as well as nepmen, and finally there were some students. Before the third siren had died away, Lesya, the inspector, Sirko and Brodsky were on the upper deck. Slowly the boat stirred and started moving away from the harbor.

A glorious summer day was beginning. The sky was clear and the Dnieper shimmered ahead with its vast waters catching the sparkling silver of the bright sun. The green banks moved by and disappeared into the blue haze of the horizon. The boat was picking p passengers on her way; theirs was the fourth stop.

Valentine had bought first-class tickets. When he was asked why he didn't buy second class, since the trip was short and there was no time even to use the cabins, he waved his hand nonchalantly and said that it was "all the same." Why pay such attention to trifles? Lesya looked at her husband and thought to herself that this was not exactly a trifling matter, since the difference in fare amounted to a day's expenses for her whole family.

As soon as he boarded the boat, Sirko kept aloof, gazing into the river. He obviously did not want to intrude upon the inspector's conversation with Lesya. Valentine, however, showing greater jealousy, did not leave Topchenko and tried to amuse him with his witticisms.

"Look at those attractive lasses!" he called out when the boat was nearing the bank and was met by a crowd of local girls. "What about you?" Valentine winked at the inspector, "Are you a lady's man?"

Topchenko realized very clearly that Valentine was tormented with jealousy, and that the reporter was doing his best to protect his wife, but at the same time the inspector felt that the balance was in his favor. Therefore, leaning sideways against Lesya he impudently replied: "Yes, you are right. I am a lady's man."

Lesya had a sick feeling around her heart. She saw that her husband was jealous of her and that Topchenko was winning in this curious game, but just now she desperately wanted to see Valentine as the victor in the struggle against the inspector. It was true that Lesya didn't value her husband very highly, but she refused to admit that he was as small as Topchenko was making him out to be. What then about Lesya herself—who had loved and esteemed Valentine but a few years previously? To admit Valentine's defeat would mean to admit her own provincialism.

She turned to Valentine and sharply, in a tone unlike any she had previously used to her husband, she said: "Valya, you mustn't be discourteous to your wife: one simply must have some feeling of human dignity."

"What are you talking about, Lesichka?" asked Brodsky, in complete ignorance.

"I mean your reference to the 'ladies.' "

Valentine started to giggle stupidly and winked at the inspector; but Topchenko looked serious and said: "Forgive us, Comrade Lesya. We did go a little too far in our conversation."

It looked as if the incident would now be closed, but the reporter suddenly felt very offended. There was really no reason why he should—except that for over an hour he had felt a great desire to explode because of his anger and dissatisfaction with the inspector's "impudent" behavior. His outburst was all the more violent therefore.

"What nonsense you are talking, Lesya! Look how innocent she is! One mustn't talk about natural desire in her company. Aren't you concerned about these things too? How on earth were your own children born? Did the stork bring them to you on its wings?"

Lesya blushed. Valentine's crudity offended her very much, but she did not say anything. The inspector was silent too. Brodsky felt no desire to continue with this argument. Having made this blunder, he once more felt his own awkwardness and, still red in the face, he went to Sirko who stood several paces away. There he sat on a chair in deep silence. The incident was finally closed.

The boat picked up a couple more passengers and steamed on southwards. The farther south it went the deeper grew the gray clouds over the horizon. It was obvious that soon these clouds would cover whatever remained of the blue sky and that there would be a storm. Neither Topchenko, nor Lesya, nor even Valentine wanted a storm. The latter had calmed down and only from time to time directed suspicious glances at Topchenko who was talking to his wife. A storm would certainly make it impossible to spend the time as planned. It is true that Bergman, the vintner, whom they were to visit, could arrange a good picnic in his house, but still such a picnic would not be the same as one spent in the open. All one could do, therefore, was to beg fortune not to let the storm ruin a good day.

"What do you think?" asked Valentine. "Is it going to rain?"

"I don't think so," replied Lesya.

"Why do you think so? Don't you see the clouds—all gathering there on the horizon?"

"Well, it won't rain simply because I don't want it to rain." Lesya turned to her husband and said, "Valya, do you think these clouds will bring rain?"

"No," snapped Valentine, coming up to his wife, "according to the weather bureau the weather will be fine for the next two weeks."

Sirko also came up, and soon a discussion on the shortcomings of our meteorology was started. Then they talked of other things; the harvest, the moods of the peasants, and the collectivization of farming. On all these subjects Topchenko showed himself so competent that Lesya couldn't help noticing his superiority over her husband and the editor. Finally the subject turned towards the vintner, Bergman, and "our" attitude to vintners. Opinions clashed. Sirko maintained that vintners did not differ at all from the kulaks, and that they should be "squeezed" a little bit more and not be given any privileges as the "center" did now. Topchenko, an expert in these matters, agreed that vintners are kulaks, but disagreed with Sirko's conclusions. Finally, when the discussion became somewhat heated, the inspector said in obvious exasperation:

"You see, forgive me for saying so, but in your arguments there is a provincial outlook. You look at our socialist construction not from a bird's eye view, but from your local belfry."

It seemed that such an outburst offered an ideal occasion for snubbing Topchenko for his superiority, but neither Sirko nor Brodsky had the courage to do it. The former made a wry face, and Valentine even forced a servile smile.

"Sure, sure," he said hastily. "We certainly view our construction from our local belfry. . . . But can you blame us for it? Wouldn't you do the same if you were living here?"

"Nobody is blaming you," replied the inspector, "but I see that you agree with me."

"Agree? What do you mean?" exclaimed Brodsky,

still all smiles. "If you will pardon the expression, you are a real demagogue."

The quarrel would have flared up again had not Lesya intervened. Realizing that Valentine was incapable of logical thought, and that any further talk would compromise him even more in the eyes of the inspector, Lesya turned her face away to the right bank, and without looking at anybody, said: "Comrades, you offend me. You are quite oblivious of my presence. What kind of gentlemen are you that not one of you has thought of offering me a glass of *kvas?* I am terribly thirsty."

Topchenko bestirred himself gallantly and, taking Lesya by the arm, said "Let me take you to the buffet. Would you like to have something to eat as well?"

"No, thank you," replied Lesya. "I just want a glass of *kvas*—here, in the fresh air."

She hoped that the inspector would leave her for a few moments and that she would then be able to exchange a few words with her husband (she wanted to tell him not to make a fool of himself). As it happened, it was Sirko who went to get the *kvas,* and so she was once more forced to witness a continuation of the same disagreeable scene.

It was now only four versts to Berestechko, with no more stops on the way. The boat was making good speed, and in a few minutes they would have to disembark. Valentine and Sirko, together with the other passengers, began to get ready and, picking up the baskets, made their way to the exit. Brodsky hoped, of course, that his wife would follow him, but nothing of the kind happened.

"We'll catch up in time," said Topchenko, keeping Lesya with him on the upper deck, "don't worry."

However, although Valentine was worried, this time he forced himself to avoid any further tactlessness by remaining behind.

"Do you drink?" Topchenko suddenly asked, remembering a scene from a novel he had read not long ago. The reporter and the editor had gone.

"Why do you want to know?" asked Lesya.

"Well, you have some *horilka* in your basket."

"No, I don't drink. We brought the *horilka* especially for the vintners. They have nothing but wine; no beer, no *horilka*. You don't drink, do you?"

"Yes, I drink." Topchenko lit a cigarette and continued to be inquisitive.

"Does your husband drink, too?"

"Why do you ask?"

"Well, nothing; I just wondered who the *horilka* is for?"

Lesya smiled. "I told you it's for the vintner." Then she suddenly added: "Are you hoping that my husband will get completely drunk?"

This last question escaped her quite unexpectedly. True, she was thinking just then that her feeble husband might in fact become quite drunk and so be utterly humiliated in the eyes of 'the Comrade from the Center,' but even then her question was really quite out of place. First, because it betrayed to the inspector her secret fears for her husband, and secondly . . . "No, no, he can't possibly think of 'that'."

But Topchenko thought precisely of 'that.'

"God forbid!" he answered. "I have no designs on you, especially if your husband should get incredibly

142

drunk."

Lesya blushed. The conversation assumed a very dangerous character. It was clear that Topchenko was paying court to her, but his manner was so crude that she couldn't help feeling offended.

"Let's go to the exit," she said, starting to walk across the deck.

But the inspector, as if nothing had happened, offered her his hand and said quietly, "Come, it'll soon be time to get off the boat."

The steamer had indeed changed course and was approaching the naked cliff around which there clustered a small crowd of people. Soon the steamer's sirens roared as it approached the jetty. "Berestechko!" called out the captain. "Who disembarks at Berestechko?"

The gangway was let down and the boat came to a halt.

III

Bergman's vineyards, to which the whole party was going, were approximately one and a half versts away, and were reached in a very short time. The visitors were met by Bergman himself, a cultured, well-mannered German. It was obvious that he knew Brodsky well, since he addressed him as his 'friend.' It was a pity, Lesya thought, that the vintner did not know how Valentine had commended him to the inspector. Bergman also knew the editor, though in talking to him he showed some coolness. As for Lesya and Topchenko, they were at once told all about Berestechko. From Bergman's warm recommendations of this little town, Lesya learned that the vintner's forefathers had come here from Switzerland as specialists in viniculture. They were brought in 1822 by the Russian government with the help of the well-known French encyclopedist, Laguerre. Having received land in the neighborhood of Akkerman, they founded their colony, Shabo, five versts away. Later, in the nineties of the last century, they learned about the Dnieper sands, came up the river and founded Berestechko.

"You cannot imagine how difficult their life was," Bergman went on, as the company finally reached his apricot orchards. "The local population met them with suspicion and hostility, and they had to battle against nature too. Not only did they have to bring the vines from Shabo in sailing boats, but the water for the vineyards also had to be brought from the Dnieper a couple of versts away, with no road to it."

Then Bergman talked of the marble beetle which systematically used to ruin the whole vine crop; of the sand which, blown by eastern winds from place to place, was a terrible scourge for the vintner; of the spring and autumn frosts, the fungi, the hail, the mists, and so on.

"It is no wonder," said he finally, "that in those circumstances many of my forefathers could not stand the life here and capitulated. Only those who were exceptionally tenacious, only the fanatics that is, surmounted all difficulties."

Sirko interjected suddenly: "All this is true; but where do you yourself come in? You speak as if of Rome, saved by the geese. Was it?"

"No, not at all," Bergman calmly replied, "we carry on our work in the vineyards with the same heroism as our forefathers. But we shall have plenty of time to talk about that . . . I take it you came here for a picnic?"

"You are right," said the inspector, who had begun to yawn after listening to the vintner's tale. "Just that—a picnic."

In an hour a tablecloth lay spread on the velvety green grass and various drinks appeared. Bergman's wife, a serious, neatly-dressed German woman, joined the company. She sat down next to her husband and silently offered food to the guests who ate and drank and, not knowing what to talk about, talked about the clouds which were still threatening a storm, but so far had failed to produce one. Soon all of the picnickers except Sirko and Lesya, were slightly tipsy. The reporter had been drinking more than the others until finally his wife tried to put an end to it by saying, "Valya, that's enough, don't you think?" But Brodsky would not stop. He went over to sit next to the inspector and was telling him of his exploits.

"Do you know the reporter Shalusky?" he asked Topchenko. "Once (that was during the old régime) he took a bet that he would interview the famous Mechnikov. Mechnikov, as you know, never gave interviews to the press. Well, you know, he won the bet. Yes! He caught the old man—sitting on the pot. Ha! Ha! Ha!"

"Why are you telling me all this?" Topchenko's sudden question struck the tipsy reporter like a heavy blow.

"Well, you know, generally speaking . . ."

"Generally speaking . . ." mockingly replied the inspector, quickly assuming a tone of authority.

145

"Can't you really think of something more interesting?" Turning to Lesya, Topchenko apologized. "Forgive me for my frankness, I simply cannot bear empty conversations."

Lesya's heart quivered as she saw that this insolent inspector had reached the peak of insolence while her Valentine was a complete numbskull. Suddenly she grasped her wineglass and drank up the contents.

"Bravo! Bravo!" shrieked Brodsky. Lesya turned to him and said very clearly: "If you only knew, Valya, why I suddenly wanted a drink, you would certainly not shout 'bravo' . . . You won't mind if I go with Comrade Topchenko to look at the vineyards?"

"By all means. I thought of going there too."

The inspector smiled, looked askance at the reporter and asked, "Aren't you jealous of your wife?"

"And what makes you think that?" asked the reporter.

"Because you won't let your wife walk with me," replied Topchenko with the same smiling look, glancing at the phlegmatic Bergman. The reporter burst into a loud, though unnatural, laugh: "Ha! Ha! you are wrong. Go on, take her for a walk. Now I'll stay here."

Brodsky had hoped, of course, that the inspector would show some tact and would apologize for the whole incident. But to his great regret, nothing of the kind happened. Topchenko only said, "That's wonderful," and taking Lesya by the arm, led her through the gates.

Berestechko slumbered in the rays of the hot southern sun; its sandy streets were empty. In the last courtyard some tireless Swiss were playing a game of croquet; otherwise everybody was resting.

"What a progressive little place," said the inspector, stopping for a while in the shade of a tree which was almost burnt up by the sun. "One can't even compare it to our villages. They consist of huts, here you see buildings; there you see drunkenness, here healthy relaxation; there dirt, here exemplary cleanliness and order. . . . Don't you agree?"

Lesya was pleased that Topchenko should seek her opinion. On such social subjects Valentine had long ceased to talk to her.

"Your comparisons," she said, "are no doubt true, although it is sad that this should be so. I never imagined that Berestechko lived such a cultured life."

"Is it possible that this is your first visit here?"

"Yes, my first visit."

"Our comrades certainly ought not to do that," Topchenko spoke with genuine indignation. "Why hasn't your husband taken you here before? From my talks with him he must have visited this place several times. . . . No, that's too bad. You must forgive me if I say that to treat one's wife in such a way is reminiscent of the old bourgeois family relationships."

Lesya smiled like a child. "Yes, you are probably right," she said. "But what can I do?"

"Well, isn't he a Party member?"

"Yes, he is."

Topchenko continued with even greater indignation and severely condemned Brodsky's behavior. This sort of thing, he indicated, was quite improper, "one can even be excluded from the Party for it."

147

At any other time Lesya would never have been so frank in her disclosures to a person she scarcely knew, and she would never have allowed Topchenko to speak to her on such a subject; but now, after Valentine's scandalous behavior, or perhaps after the wine, she listened to the inspector with great satisfaction.

"You must forgive me once more for saying so," said Topchenko, pressing his elbow against Lesya's hand, "but I just could not live like that."

Lesya trembled. Having seen the kindness in Topchenko's eyes and his sincere compassion for her, she realized that he was the man she had dreamed about last night. Topchenko, as if guessing that, pressed himself even closer to her, but at that very moment Bergman crossed their path.

"So I have caught up with you by taking a short cut," he said. "You are going the wrong way. The finest vineyards are on this side."

Both Lesya and the inspector were displeased with the vintner's appearance, but naturally, they did not show it and, thanking him for his trouble they walked on in the direction he indicated.

"I haven't finished telling you," said Bergman, returning to their interrupted conversation—for he had come here to renew it—"Comrade Sirko doesn't trust me or my fellow vintners, but as a matter of fact all I care about is not myself or my friends but the state."

Here Bergman took up the story of how well the vintners had acquitted themselves during the Civil War, with what efforts they had helped to organize co-operatives, etc. So he simply could not understand why he and his fellow vintners should have been deprived of the vote. "This disfranchisement," said Bergman, "has ruined the co-operative organization, since those who were deprived of the vote have also been excluded from the co-operatives."

"You should inform the center about it," Topchenko yawned.

"We did," replied Bergman wiping the sweat off his forehead. "The relation of the Soviet government to us. . . ." Here the vintner began to enumerate all those persons of authority who had visited Berestechko and who had been "so nice" to him. Then he took up one of the main issues:

"Just think," he said, "according to official statistics, a worker in the Daghestan Republic, let us say, earns fifty kopeks a day, while the average price-index is one ruble. On the other hand, with our system of seventeen grades of workers, the workers of the first grade earn eighteen rubles. Is this right in your opinion?"

"I have no opinion on the matter," said the inspector, yawning once more and glancing at Lesya who, her eyes glistening after the wine, was walking in a kind of daze. "Could you explain it a little more?"

"Certainly. I have already told you about the norms in Daghestan. Now compare them with ours. A skilled pruner here gets two rubles forty-eight kopeks plus twenty-seven per cent, that is, another sixty-seven kopeks (made up of sixteen per cent for insurance, five and a half per cent for the workers' committee and its cultural work, one per cent for the home of rest, a half per cent for the scholarship fund, a half per cent for building the peoples' home, rent of office for the workers' committee—three per cent; all in all, twenty-seven per cent); that is two rubles forty-eight kopeks plus sixty-seven kopeks, giving a total of three rubles fifteen kopeks. Women helpers get one ruble eighty-kopeks plus twenty-seven per cent—that is forty-eight kopeks—two rubles twenty-five kopeks. Hours . . ."

The vintner showed no sign of stopping. However, when he compared present prices with pre-war ones, saying that before the war he paid a pruner only one ruble, Lesya turned to him with a protest: "So before the war he got a ruble; now he gets two rubles forty-eight kopeks (he never actually receives the twenty seven per cent you mentioned). Do you really think that this shows such an increase, especially in view of the fact that the ruble's value before the war was higher and that the revolution was fought for the benefit of the workers and peasants?"

"Quite right, quite right," fluttered the vintner. "But you must put yourself in our position."

However, Lesya, usually so composed, this time refused to 'put herself in his position,' and having thanked Bergman for his information, she politely took her leave and walked on with Topchenko.

The scorching mid-day sun was beginning to decline, but the heat was still intense. The sky was cloudless; not a bird flew in the air; it was as if everything was dead. The sandy dunes stretched out on the right and seemed endless in this limitless steppe. But for occasional vines scattered here and there in clumps, it would seem not a steppe on the

Dnieper's bank, but the Sahara desert. It was unbearable to go any further, and so Lesya and the inspector made their way to the Dnieper. As soon as they set foot on its high bank, a cool breeze blew against them. The conversation was once more directed to a discussion of Valentine's relationship with his wife.

"Yes, indeed, it reminds one of the old family relationships," repeated the inspector, sitting down beside Lesya who had found some shade and was sitting on the grassy river bank. "To be quite frank, I think you are an ideal woman. . . . Such women are only to be found in the provinces."

Lesya realized that Topchenko was simply paying her compliments and that when he went back to Kharkiv he would forget her the next day. And yet she was pleased to hear him talk like this—she could listen to his talk almost without end.

"You know," continued Topchenko at the same time leaning inadvertently, as it were, against Lesya's shoulder, "I never have any luck with women. You wonder, of course, why I tell you this. Frankly, I envy your husband."

Lesya realized that the inspector, though not perhaps lying outright, was exaggerating somewhat, and yet she liked to listen to him. No matter how impudent and arrogant he might be—yet there was just no comparison between him and her provincial and petty Valentine. How painful it was for Lesya to watch her husband today. So painful that she would have liked to drink more wine in order to let her head swim even more and her heart beat even quicker.

She did so on her way to join Bergman. Accompanied by Topchenko, she called at a vineyard and drank another bottle of wine. She was not mistaken about the result. The world unfolded itself before her eyes in the most ravishing colors. Lesya had expected (for she did think of that too) that Valentine would greet her with an angry look. But the jealous reporter, having lost all confidence in himself and not knowing how to put an end to the inspector's flirtation with his wife, had drunk so much 'out of woe' that now he was lying in Bergman's orchard —dead drunk. Lesya and Topchenko were also told that the taciturn Sirko, to escape from his solitude, had gone to the harbor and thence by motorboat back home.

"So that's that," commented Topchenko. "You all looked forward to this picnic, and now the whole thing, if you will forgive the expression, has fizzled out. Is this how you in the provinces always arrange your picnics?" The inspector said this in an injured voice, but even the tipsy Lesya could see that he was really quite pleased with the news; she was glad to be able to spend another hour or two in the inspector's company. She tried to hide her emotion, however, deep in her fluttering heart.

"Well," said Topchenko, "all that is left for us to do is to thank our host for his reception and go to the harbor. When does the boat arrive?"

"It can be here in an hour or in three hours," replied Bergman, "that depends on Kherson."

"Then we had better start off now; I must leave for Kharkiv today."

IV

They had some trouble with Valentine who couldn't get up, swore, and did not recognize anyone. Bergman's help alone made it possible to get him to the harbor. There he stretched himself out on the grass and fell asleep. In a moment he woke up, put two fingers into his mouth, left a pool beside him and fell asleep again.

"How revolting," remarked Lesya, looking at her husband with disgust.

"There is nothing very attractive here," agreed Topchenko, suggesting to Lesya that they sit down in the shade of a nearby oak.

They sat there for nearly an hour and a half, but the boat did not appear. Another hour passed; it began to grow dark, and still there was no sign of the boat. The sun had set, a lighthouse gleamed along the distant waters of the Dnieper, and the stars were out. Groups of village boys and girls were singing and dancing not far from the harbor. The boat was still overdue and Valentine showed no sign of returning life.

"How unreal everything seems now—the harbor, the stars and sky, the air, the Dnieper—all of it. Don't you feel that?" asked Lesya.

"Yes, I do," replied Topchenko placing his hand on Lesya's arm.

"You know," Lesya went on as if dreaming. "I think that all the troubles of mankind are due to the fact that there are so many provincials. If everyone lived in a city like Kharkiv, then they would not suffer as I do now, for provincial life narrows the horizon."

"Yes, especially in a family like yours," Topchenko added carefully.

Lesya suddenly turned to the inspector and said: "No, be frank, you won't offend me. It's men like Valentine that narrow that horizon." Lesya sighed and then added: "Yes, Comrade, I want to be quite frank too. You see it hurts me so much to see that my Valya cannot behave in public the way . . . for instance, that you can."

Topchenko raised his hand in protest. Surely his own weaknesses were many and he could not be held up as an example of the perfect man. However, all this was said in a tone in which self-criticism was but a thin disguise for parading his modesty. Lesya only saw the modesty, not the ostentation, perhaps because the wine had affected her and the night was so wonderful, except, of course, for the tipsy Valentine.

The boat was very late, and left Berestechko at ten o'clock. Valentine again proved quite a problem. After getting permission from the captain of the boat, they carried Valya into a cabin. There he fell asleep instantaneously. Lesya and Topchenko were left on the deck.

Moonlight poured over the earth. The waters of the Dnieper sparkled like diamonds and churned under the paddle of the boat.

Everything was still and only a light breeze caressed their faces. The upper deck was deserted, so that Lesya and Topchenko were left together.

"I understand you," said the inspector, again pressing against Lesya with his shoulder, "and I see how unhappy you are. With your personality and temperament you should never live in this mud. You should live . . ." The inspector gently pressed Lesya's hand. She, not seeing anyone near, returned the pressure, although she felt her face flushing suddenly.

"You are so beautiful," the inspector went on, "you . . ."

There the familiar story began: the intoxicated husband lay unconscious and his tipsy and frustrated wife accepted the advances of another man, who although almost a stranger, was yet not unattractive to her. A moment later the inspector was already embracing Lesya and then he rushed to kiss her. Now they were both silent, looking carefully to see whether they could be seen or surprised by anyone. There was no need to be alarmed. The first class lounge was empty, the deck too was deserted. The second and third classes were half occupied and most of the travellers were now resting in their cabins. . . . From the third class deck they could hear a faint and melancholy song sung by a girl who was going somewhere north. Probably Lesya herself could not have explained why she had succumbed to Topchenko's ardor so quickly; he, on the other hand, was quite aware that if it were not for the wine and Valentine's disgraceful behavior, all his wooing would have been in vain. All the more, therefore, did he try to make the most of this opportunity. Not only did he kiss Lesya constantly, but becoming even bolder, he proposed in a whisper that she should "come down to his cabin to lie down for a while."

"What are you talking about?" Lesya said indignantly, but she felt no indignation herself and thought

that she would go to Topchenko's cabin and that
which her jealous husband was so much afraid
of when he tried to stop her from going for a walk
with the inspector, would happen in that cabin.
"What are you thinking of?" she repeated.

"Lesichka," whispered Topchenko, who was "thou-
ing" her now, "why don't you? Is it because you love
your husband?"

"Yes, I love him. Don't talk to me about it. I shall
not go with you."

Lesya was still 'youing' the inspector and resisting
him. But somehow both of them knew that her resistance would crumble and that she would come.
Finally, when Lesya's face was aflame from Topchenko's kisses, she said in a trembling voice: "All
right, I'll come. Only you go first and see if Valya is
still asleep."

Topchenko hurriedly walked off to the reporter's
cabin. Lesya was left alone. She leaned against the
railing; her whole body trembled. It seemed that
there was really nothing bad or unusual moving her,
and yet she realized that she was doing something
terrible, unatonable, and criminal.

The boat was rapidly turning northward. . . .
Ploughing through the quiet Dnieper, it paddled
rhythmically upstream. The moon was reflected in
myriads of diamonds on the river's surface. The sky
line was dim; from time to time the flash of a distant
lighthouse bubbled up. The banks could no longer
be seen; they melted into the surrounding darkness
and only when the boat had passed close to one of
them could the blurred silhouettes of dark trees be
discerned.

Topchenko quickly returned and embracing Lesya told her that Valentine was sound asleep.

"Are you quite sure?" she asked in a wavering tone.

"Yes, we can be sure of that."

All that was left now was to go to the inspector's cabin, but Lesya still hesitated to go and asked— "Do you realize what we are about to do?"

"Yes, I do."

"And aren't you afraid?" Lesya was shaking like a leaf. "Aren't you afraid? I must tell you—I am— terribly scared."

"Really, Lesichka!" said the inspector, embracing her once more, "That's sheer philistinism."

"Are you sure of that?"

"Yes, quite sure."

"What if I become pregnant—have you thought of that?"

Topchenko didn't like Lesya's behavior. Being an impatient man he tried to trick her since he could wait no longer.

"Well, if you are afraid, then don't come."

"No," Lesya said quietly, "I want to and I am not afraid any more."

The inspector took her by the hand and pulled her gently towards his cabin. They had taken no more than a couple of paces when they met someone. They halted. Both Lesya and the inspector thought it was Valentine. The inspector was preparing something to say and Lesya, burning with the fire of purity, had decided to tell her husband the whole truth—that she didn't love him, that he was ridiculous, that she could not go on living with him. She had even decided to ask him not to prevent her from abandoning herself to Topchenko. Such thoughts flashed like lightning through Lesya's head; they even calmed her a little. But when the figure approached them they saw that it was not Valentine. They couldn't see his face, but he appeared taller than Valentine. Their meeting, however, was not without sequel. The man, who was about to pass them suddenly, called out:

"Is that you, Topchenko?"

"Yes," answered the inspector, and dropping Lesya's hand ran to the man. . . . . "Semen Petrovich? Well, I didn't expect to see you here."

"Why are you here?" the man whom the inspector called Semen Petrovich asked sternly. "I thought you were to be back in Kharkiv long ago."

The inspector squirmed. It was obvious that the person he had met was his boss. He tried bluffing, but managed it very clumsily and now he looked not unlike the reporter as he had appeared during the day. Possibly his behavior was even more humiliating than Brodsky's and Sirko's. Without any apology to Lesya, he left her and walked away with his Semen Petrovich as if she had never been there.

"Semen Petrovich," the inspector whined, "I give you my word of honor that I came here on business . . . I. . . ."

But Lesya was listening no longer. The encounter had so overwhelmed her that all of a sudden she became quite sober, but a moment later, seeing that Topchenko had gone, she felt a strange pain in her breast. It ached not so much because of what could have happened and had not, after all, happened, but because the man whom she had thought to be exceptional and belonging to a class apart from her Valentine had turned out to be an ordinary bureaucrat, and even perhaps inferior to her husband.

"And that was the man to whom I wanted to give myself," Lesya thought bitterly.

All at once she saw life in its real, not its imaginary colors and she realized that people are always almost ridiculously the same. Lesya leaned over the railing and looked into the distance. It was dim; only very, very far away on the horizon, probably near Kichkass, one could see the lighthouse. Lesya was deep in thought.

Five minutes later the inspector came running back and putting his hand on Lesya's shoulder, said: "Forgive me, Lesichka, I met my boss and was obliged to . . . Well, I'm free now, let's go."

In silence Lesya removed Topchenko's hand from her shoulder, looked into his eyes, and leaning over the railing began to cry softly.

———

Translated by G. and M. Luckyj.

IVAN IVANOVICH

Why portray the poverty and imperfection of life, digging people out
from the wilds, from the most distant
corners of the country? But this cannot be helped, if such is the character
of the author; if he is so sick at heart
over his own imperfection, and if he
can portray only the poverty and imperfection of life, digging people out
from the wilds and the remotest
corners of the country! Now once
more we find ourselves back in such
a corner. But what a wilderness and
what a corner!

GOGOL

Thackeray, writing of Swift's death, says that so
great a man he seemed that thinking of him was like
thinking of an empire falling. Ivan Ivanovich would
certainly have agreed with this especially when he was
expelled from the third-year law course at College
for "Voltairean tendencies." It was then that he
promised, in the event of the victory of the "revo-

lutionary masses," to display *Gulliver's Travels* as one of his favorite books and to place it on the right hand of Rabelais, whose *Gargantua and Pantagruel* he bought for next to nothing in a second-hand bookstore.

However, all this happened a long time ago, and since then Ivan Ivanovich had simply forgotten that Swift ever existed. True enough, his nice youngster is growing rapidly and one day, you never know, he may take a fancy to the malevolent English satirist and thus show once more a "Voltairean tendency." However, this story is about the father, not about the son. Forgive me, therefore, this slight digression, or, rather, ornate introduction, and let us approach the main theme.

* * *

My hero, a nice fellow, lives in Thomas More Street. In itself it is not a bad spot, situated in the hilly part of our, as Ivan Ivanovich would put it in his derision of the bourgeois middle class, "out-and-out revolutionary" town. Here you can see asphalt on the pavement and on the street itself, along which taxis race gingerly and antediluvian hansom cabs trail slowly and sadly. In front of almost every house you can see beautiful flower beds which, in the summer, breathe out the sweet fragrance of mignonette. Many years ago this street was called Governor Street and was full of the busybody officials of the Imperial regime. Now however, as Methody Kirilovich, whom I shall introduce to you later, would tell you, not one of these officials could be seen on the pavement. The point is, of course, that, as my hero would remark,

161

Thomas More Street presents a picture of exemplary order in a "new revolutionary interpretation." There is therefore nothing strange in the fact that Ivan Ivanovich lives in this model district instead of in some other place still reminiscent of the old regime.

The house in which Ivan Ivanovich lives also has its obvious advantages. It was built only two years ago and its proletarian origin is thus beyond doubt. It is true that the construction of this skyscraper was connected with some shady business, but to begin with, this detail has nothing to do with our story, and secondly who could believe that the architect, discharged after the worker and peasant inspection, had any connection with the old city council which, as everybody knows, was the seat of robbers and speculators. Thus the house too is in accordance with the progressive views of my hero.

"Good evening, Ivan Ivanovich, how are you?"

"Oh, how are you, Hippolit Onufrievich? As you see, I am just on my way back from the meeting. . . ."

My hero walks along the street solemnly, as only very worthy and upright citizens can walk. The brilliant sun is skipping like a hare along the window panes of the pleasant houses; it gives him its blessing on his difficult path. However, as it will take him another half-hour to reach his home, let us get there ahead of him and introduce to you his family, the family that is "creating the communist reality."

Let us walk slowly into the house and find the apartment in question. First door—no. Second door —no. At last, number 38, and at once the smell of fresh eau de Cologne.

Unfortunately, only my hero's wife, Marfa Halaktionovna, is in. Her nickname in Party circles, by the way, is Comrade Halakta. Marfa Halaktionovna is also a very nice woman and this, too, is in accordance with the progressive views of Ivan Ivanovich, who, by the way, is called Jean by Party members. Marfa Halaktionovna, to mention only a few of her virtues, never has manicures, except on very rare occasions, for hygiene's sake, as she explains. She dresses simply yet with taste, and is certainly not as extravagant as the so-called *nepmanki*.[1] She is not slim and slender, but to be truthful, of medium height with an inclination to opulence. Her black, elegantly cut hair, arranged with the praiseworthy intention of enabling other Party members to call her "Comrade Halakta" during Party meetings while remaining Marfa Halaktionovna at home, is surely the characteristic feature of a woman of the new regime. True, she is shrewder than her husband, yet this must be regarded purely as a biological fact having nothing to do with social changes.

Marfa Halaktionovna loves to read Lenin and Marx. Sometimes, though, when she sits down to read Lenin and Marx, her hand stretches out involuntarily for a volume of de Maupassant. This usually happens when a fresh vernal breeze, so lovely and yet so unsubordinated to the monumental-realist theory, steals into her room, even into her bosom. Yet even then Comrade Halakta manages to keep herself in hand. At such a time she finds escape in novels like "Julio Jurenito" with a preface by Buk-

---

[1] Wives of officials benefiting under the New Economic Policy.

harin or "The Love Story of Jeanne Ney" without a preface by Bukharin but with one by some author whose other works have been prefaced by members of the Central Committee of the Communist Party.

Comrade Halakta and Ivan Ivanovich have one son and one daughter. They gave their son a revolutionary name—May, and their daughter a no less revolutionary one—Violet. May has already enrolled as an "Octobrist," [2] Violet is only a candidate.

Apart from the "acknowledged" members of the family there are also those, so to speak, "unacknowledged" ones; those unconnected by intimate family ties. They are Mademoiselle Lucy, the governess, and Yavdokha, a Soviet cook and a member of the local trade union. Hence the proportion of servants to masters in Ivan Ivanovich's household is two to four. In other words, quite a lawful proportion, having nothing to do with bourgeois traditions.

But who is this Ivan Ivanovich? My hero has just come home and put his umbrella away in the bright spot made by the sun which blesses with its pink and white rays his difficult, daily path. Whoever is this Ivan Ivanovich?

Good heavens, isn't it obvious yet? According to Semen Yakovich (about him you will learn later) Ivan Ivanovich is an exemplary member of such and such a board, or of such and such a trust. It is true that his salary is two hundred and fifty karbovantsi, but one can speak of this amount only when one does not count such various small items as overtime pay and the regular honorarium which he receives

---

[2] First grade of Communist youth training.

from the local press for writing articles that are not exactly original. My hero's financial situation is therefore below the average if one considers the budget of a contemporary bourgeois or the rate of exchange of chervonets and especially the fact that Ivan Ivanovich is a man with (almost) a higher education.

Comrade Jean (Ivan Ivanovich) always wipes his forehead and his rimmed glasses with a snow-white handkerchief and speaks in a bass-baritone voice. Having learned English wisdom in matters of economy he wears a suit that is certainly not cheap.

"I am not so rich," says my hero, "as to be able to afford a cheap suit."

"It is so obvious," confirms Marfa Halaktionovna, "only our primitive people don't think of that."

"Don't they really?" says Comrade Jean, looking over his glasses at his wife and straightening the vest which covers his uncomfortably distended stomach.

Marfa Halaktionovna does not care to answer such questions and closing her eyes she lies down on the sofa. A bird looking exactly like a canary, sits on the windowsill and sings "chirik-chirik." Just then Yavdokha, the cook, starts humming in the kitchen, but her chant is hardly intelligible. The song seems to be pitched in a major key, but still it jars occasionally:

> .... People talk of something new
> A purge will catch up with you....

Comrade Halakta is thinking: how strange, how difficult it is to understand the fact that the common people are still dissatisfied and cannot live joyously. This damned heritage of tsardom.

Ivan Ivanovich again looks at his wife from over his glasses and glancing towards the kitchen door where Yavdokha is working, asks his wife in a scarcely audible voice, "Well, Halaktochka . . . and what do they say of me?"

"Say where?"

"Well, generally, so to speak, in Party circles, and generally, everywhere."

Comrade Halakta looks at Comrade Jean with a motherly expression and says "What else can they say about you? They say you are a very good worker and an exemplary Party member."

Ivan Ivanovich rubs his hands, walks up to the radio and strokes its smooth surface tenderly. He is completely satisfied with this information. The main thing is that there should be no misunderstanding. Is he not ready to face death for the sake of the Party and socialist construction? No wonder, therefore, that Comrade Halakta overhears his name mentioned, as it always is, without blemish in all sorts of conversations.

"Halaktochka," asks Ivan Ivanovich, taking out a card from his pocket, "isn't it tomorrow that the contribution to the 'Friends of the Children' is due?"

"Why are you in such a hurry?" answers Marfa Halaktionovna. "You are far too anxious. Some people don't pay for five months, and you never let a month go by."

"That's how it should be. I must set an example for others, especially for the backward non-Party masses."

"That's true enough," says Marfa Halaktionovna "but isn't it vexing to know that this little heroism on your part will not even be noticed, let alone put down to your credit?"

My hero waves his snow white hand abruptly:

"That doesn't matter. I don't want to have my selfless actions noticed. That is how the standard of Communism should be borne!"

Ivan Ivanovich walks over to the window, opens it and his eyes wander far away in deep meditation. Beyond the garden's end he sees where quiet fields and soft sky begin, where wonderful horizons enchant the soul with a quiet yearning that doesn't stir one to rebel in the spirit of petty bourgeois impressionism, but, on the contrary, calms one with the joyous peace of monumental realism.

"It doesn't matter," repeats Ivan Ivanovich almost unconsciously, spreading wide his arms towards this most beautiful horizon and breathing in with dilated nostrils the scent of the mignonette from the first "workers' and peasants' flower bed."

In such moments the utter devotion of my hero reaches its peak. One feels like lowering the flag of the Republic before such devotion and saying with deep satisfaction: "Ivan Ivanovich, you are indeed the model man of our unparalleled epoch. Your name is sure to figure in the Red Pantheon!"

In fact, who else pays his membership dues as promptly as my hero does? It is true that they do not amount to two per cent of his earnings, but what matters is quantity not quality. And quantity is obvious here all right. He is a member of the "Friends of the Children," of the "Air Fleet," and of the "Society for the Development of the Chemical Industry." He belongs to a club of former political prisoners, for true enough, during the old regime it was my hero whom they wanted to deport from one county to another; he is a member of the local trade union, etc., etc. Altogether, in this respect Ivan Ivanovich has no peer.

Besides, his propaganda for a wide membership has been successful even in the case of his wife, Marfa Halaktionovna, whom he has managed to enlighten as to the value of selflessness and the small unpublicized heroisms in the midst of the stormy life of our "out-and-out revolutionary" town.

"Yet," Ivan Ivanovich sighs finally as he sits down on the sofa, "one thing I just cannot understand."

"What is it, Jean?" asks Marfa Halaktionovna.

"Well, you know, this whole business of socialist construction."

"Are you beginning to have doubts?" asks Marfa Halaktionovna in a lowered voice, looking to see if there is anyone to overhear them in the next room.

"However can you say such things?" gesticulates my hero nervously. "What do you take me for? No! I simply cannot understand those. . . . What shall I call them? . . . our opponents. What do they want? What do they want from us? Well now, let us ask ourselves: Is there a dictatorship of the proletariat? Yes, there is! Is the power in our hands? Yes, it is! Have the factories been nationalized? Yes, they have! Is there a Red Army? Yes, there is! Is there a Komintern? Yes, there is! Is there a Profintern? Yes, there is!"

Ivan Ivanovich pauses for a moment, takes out of his pocket a snow-white handkerchief and after wiping off his glasses he continues—"Let us go further

Is there universal education? Yes, there is! Are we approaching socialism? Yes, we are! Is there a Komsomol? Yes, there is! And the Pioneers? Yes, they too. What else do they want? I simply cannot understand."

Marfa Halaktionovna straightens her bodice and with half-closed eyes that are so wise, says, "What do they want? They don't want anything. All this is merely a matter of personal squabbles. Purely a struggle behind the scenes."

"Even so, even so," Ivan Ivanovich gets more and more excited and his baritone voice begins to ascend towards the treble. "I can forgive ordinary Party members for such degenerate thoughts—but the leaders!" My hero here makes a most emphatic gesture. "I cannot tolerate this in our leaders. That's just how I'm made. They can beg me on their knees, they can do what they like to me, I simply cannot tolerate it."

Ivan Ivanovich runs across the room, waves his hands and looks persistently at a particular spot on the floor. It seems that there he sees one of the leaders." And this leader is kneeling down, begging mercy from Ivan Ivanovich.

"That's enough," says Marfa Halaktionovna, "don't get excited, Jean. I am worried about your heart."

But Ivan Ivanovich can't calm down. He walks over to the window, breathes deeply the sweet scent of the mignonette and as if in a trance, continues, "Heart? How can I care about my heart when the interests of the proletariat are at stake? I don't like to parade my devotion, I don't engage in flowery oratory at Party meetings or in the Press. But at least in my own home allow me to open my soul and to pour out what boils in it. You may think there is little there, but believe me. . . ."

Here Ivan Ivanovich begins to feel that his heart has really let him down. He sinks down on to the sofa and asks for a glass of water.

"God Almighty," cries out Marfa Halaktionovna running to fetch a decanter. "You have upset me again. Shall I send for the doctor? And all because of these damned controversies."

"Please, don't bother, darling. I am all right." Ivan Ivanovich closes his eyes. "I can't help being so emotional, having such a Bolshevik temperament. But what else can I do? I cannot regard the degeneration of the Party with indifference."

In a moment my hero gets up and walks to his study. Comrade Halakta comes over to the window and as she gazes out into the garden she sees her young son and daughter passing the flower beds.

"Vous aimez les fleurs, Mademoiselle Lucy?" asks Marfa Halaktionovna.

"Comment donc, madame!" replies Mademoiselle.

Somebody knocks at the door and in a moment in walks Methody Kirilovich, a close friend of Ivan Ivanovich. Methody Kirilovich looks like a mouse. His eyes keep darting about, his hands move constantly, and his whole figure is very much alive. Comrade Halakta once said that she liked Methody Kirilovich because of his slyly arched eyebrows and his wise head.

"Please be quiet," says Marfa Halaktionovna, "Jean is terribly upset and he must have a good rest. Let's leave him in his study for a while."

Methody Kirilovich kisses his hostess's hand and

informs her that he's only dropped in for a few moments. Then they sit down on the sofa and begin to discuss the problem of sex.

"It is an undisputed fact," says Marfa Halaktionovna with half-closed eyes and a sigh, "that, as far as the common people are concerned, we have solved this cursed problem of sex. At least, let us say, in principle, and in this respect bourgeois science must capitulate before Marxism. But then, you know, there are those exceptional individuals to whom sex remains a riddle."

"You are thinking of yourself, of course," smiles Methody Kirilovich with his sly eyebrows and quite unintentionally, but accidentally and almost unconsciously, he places his hand on Marfa Halaktionovna's attractive waist.

"I cannot tell lies," sighs Marfa Halaktionovna. "I tell you frankly and without any petty bourgeois prejudices. You cannot imagine what a great desire I have at times to caress strange men."

Methody Kirilovich looks at the door leading to the study and drawing much closer to Marfa Halaktionovna begins to stroke her knee.

"You just cannot imagine," whispers Marfa Halaktionovna. "It is such . . . how shall I put it? Such a violent desire that . . ."

Methody Kirilovich begins to shake nervously. At this point the author walks with decision to the door. Being a satirist, his work is naturally not successful with some of the important people in the Republic. Not without good reason, these important people point out that satire has outlived its usefulness and that in our society there is no room for satire. However, let me assure you of one thing. We do not listen to what must not be overheard and we do not spy on what must not be seen.

II

The apartment in which Ivan Ivanovich lives with his family consists only (only!) of four rooms, not counting the kitchen and the bathroom. It comprises a study, a dining room, the children's bedroom, and a bedroom for my hero and his wife. Thus it is obvious that the housing crisis has made itself felt here and that my hero has faced it courageously. Ivan Ivanovich never, for instance, demanded that his cook should have a separate bedroom. Hence Yavdokha sleeps on a bed in the hallway. Indeed by what right could he claim another room? It is true that he would be pleased to know that his cook had a corner of her own. However, he is an enlightened Party member and knows well how others have to live. Many are in a far worse position, some have only three rooms, Mykola Hryhorovich for instance.

"Do you think that everyone has a four-room apartment?" he asks his wife.

"You know they haven't," says Marfa Halaktionovna emphatically. "If they had there would be no housing shortage. Some have three, others only two rooms."

Ivan Ivanovich smiles with satisfaction. "So I am right again," says he, "the feeling of proletarian equality is very strong in me."

My hero walks up to the bust of a well-known Marxist (there are several such busts in this room) and lingers in meditation over this, as he would say "old chieftain." His eyes wander to other pieces of furniture in the room. He is remembering the stormy days, the days of the swift and fiery Red Cavalry, of the world conflagration in the West, when he would not have believed that one day he would lead a comparatively peaceful proletarian existence, surrounded by hostile bourgeois states. Those were the days when Ivan Ivanovich selflessly shed his blood for a better future by working together with Comrade Halakta on the board of the People's Educational Committee. It was then that he received some of this furniture, as a surprise gift from his colleagues. The furniture still preserves its modern look today and this again is in accord with my hero's modern outlook on life.

It consists of six or seven Turkish rugs, a Becker grand piano, a dozen Viennese stools, a scientific library, an oak desk completely equipped, a large dining table, several spring mattresses, etc. In truth, I do not know how much of this furniture was actually paid for, but I do know that Ivan Ivanovich, being a modest man, does not like to flaunt this gift which was meant to be a surprise. To be sure he still preserves some feeling of gratitude towards his colleagues, but on the other hand it is no secret that at the time of the communist household inventory my hero almost renounced his gift. The matter was finally settled through Marfa Halaktionovna's intervention.

"Very well," she said then, "let's admit that your colleagues, who gave you this furniture as a gift, did in fact requisition it from some landowner. But first of all, was this an easy matter? Couldn't they have been slain by counterrevolutionaries then and there? And secondly, why should we really bother? Didn't we have to leave all our property to those white bandits? And could we possibly remember now what was given to us and what we bought?"

Ivan Ivanovich wasn't quite sure what his actual property was, but being a determined man and not a sentimentalist he said, while noticing a strange bird against the tender blue sky, to the official taking down the inventory, "Sure, take everything down! I cannot possibly remember now what I bought and what I received as a gift."

"Well then," said the official, "how can I make an inventory, if you don't remember which were the pieces of furniture you were entitled to?"

Ivan Ivanovich blushed. The whole story was so sordid to him. Surely nobody could ever question his honesty, and yet this silly situation put him in such a ridiculous position that he felt like falling through the floor. "No, please, take down everything," energetically repeated my devoted hero. "You see, the gift is from my colleagues and I am not sure whether there are some requisitioned articles too."

"Let us see, then, which are the things you bought."

"I can't possibly remember," cried out Ivan Ivanovich quite sincerely, "take down everything."

"If that's the case, then I'd better leave you as you are," said the official, himself a little confused, and quickly left the room.

Thus, against his will, Ivan Ivanovich found himself surrounded by gifts. And so he begins each one of his days on the, so to speak, "surprise" mattress.

* * *

It is one of those days during the working season. The autumn rains drive, as if on purpose, all sorts of grumblers against Ivan Ivanovich. His Communist cell gathers regularly once a week, though nobody is keen to preside over the Thursday meeting, for it is not yet known whether there will or will not be a new purge.

Ivan Ivanovich wakes up, feeling happy and satisfied, in an appropriately monumental-realistic mood. With half-closed eyes he looks at Marfa Halaktionovna. She is sound asleep and dreaming, of course, of the old rebellious days and her work in the People's Office of Education. Ivan Ivanovich gives her another look, then tickles her. Marfa Halaktionovna jerks her leg and wakes up suddenly.

"Well, what are we going to have for lunch today?" asks Ivan Ivanovich, smiling happily, though with restraint.

Comrade Halakta yawns, slowly sits up and ruffles her hair. "And what do you suggest?" she asks. Ivan Ivanovich produces another of his self-confident smiles. "And what do you think?" he says, "Guess what I should like?"

"I think you are going to suggest another bourgeois menu," grumbles Marfa Halaktionovna.

"You are wrong," exclaims Ivan Ivanovich gleefully. "Nothing of the kind. Being what I am, I just could not invent a bourgeois menu."

"Well, let's have your suggestion, then," says Marfa Halaktionovna still discontented.

"I have an idea," continues Ivan Ivanovich. "You make a good little Russian borshch, then we won't have a second course, and let's have a jelly for dessert."

"How fantastic," comments Marfa Halaktionovna. "It is impossible not to have a second course."

At this point Ivan Ivanovich asks his wife not to get excited and tells her that yesterday he saw freshly smoked fish in the store, so fresh it made your mouth water. So he thought he would buy a couple and also a small bottle of Armenian vodka. Surely this would do for the second course. "What do you think, darling?" asks Ivan Ivanovich.

"I am sure that smoked fish and a bottle of Armenian will do as a second course for you," answers Marfa Halaktionovna. "But what about the children and Mademoiselle Lucy?"

My hero directs an angry look towards the children's bedroom. "It won't hurt Mademoiselle Lucy to eat freshly smoked fish," he says decisively. "Really, you are conventional: it is impossible not to have a second course. No! And besides, Halaktochka, you are not very good at giving the servants a true proletarian upbringing. You know how easy it is to descend to a bourgeois level."

"Wait," interrupts Marfa Halaktionovna. "First of all, I am not thinking of Mademoiselle Lucy so much as of the children. What shall they have for a second course? Smoked fish and vodka as well?"

"Yes, that's true," says Ivan Ivanovich with a resigned gesture. "They will have to have cutlets."

So we see that for lunch today there will be no second course. Lunch will consist of Little Russian borshch, jelly, smoked fish, the Armenian vodka (my hero is a very moderate drinker), and cutlets. The cutlets will not count as a second course. They will

176

be for the children and, of course, for all the others, except Ivan Ivanovich who does not care much for them.

The menu, prepared according to the proper ideology, is thus complete. A day has begun in the household of Ivan Ivanovich. A heavy truck is just passing noisily under the windows and from far away there comes the cheerful cry of the passionate siren which gladdens the hearts of all citizens. Ivan Ivanovich goes to the office. Marfa Halaktionovna gives orders to Yavdokha and Mademoiselle Lucy.

"Why are you so late today, Yavdokha?" asks Marfa Halaktionovna on her way to the kitchen.

"I went to my union first," answers the cook.

Marfa Halaktionovna raises her eyebrows. Sure, she has nothing against Trade Unions; on the contrary, she is in favor of them. But one should do things in a proper manner. Couldn't she have told her mistress about it in advance?

"You must understand," says Comrade Halakta. "You yourself know how much I am doing to help you. It is really my slogan, you know, that every cook should be fit to be a People's Commissar. But I can't put up with anarchy. You must understand that. In that way we cannot build socialism. I could have dismissed you for what you have done, but I won't do it. I know you would not be able to find any other work these days."

Marfa Halaktionovna speaks in such a sincere and moving tone that Yavdokha finally agrees with her that she did wrong, and understanding that one cannot build socialism in such a way, she begs forgiveness.

After this lecture in political education Marfa Halaktionovna goes to the dining room where Mademoiselle Lucy and the children are drinking tea.

"And how is my Violet? Is she eating well?" asks Marfa Halaktionovna.

"A la bonne heure, madame," answers Mademoiselle Lucy.

Comrade Halakta gives the children a motherly look and says in the soft voice of a social educator, "Well, how did you sleep, my children? Do you feel well?"

Violet, too small to understand what her mother is talking about, sticks her finger into her nose, but the four-year-old May informs his mother eagerly: "Oui, oui, maman."

"That's splendid," says Marfa Halaktionovna. "One should always be happy, my children. You must not forget that there are thousands of homeless children—out on the streets. Such children are far worse off. They don't even have a home and run about the streets like stray puppies. You mustn't forget them."

"Oui, oui," says May in a confident and happy voice as if he understood.

Marfa Halaktionovna then suggests that Mademoiselle Lucy should take the children into the kindergarten for an hour and a half. May and Violet, she thinks, must not lose touch with collective life. Only in a group can a child develop properly. The governess takes May and Violet by their hands and leads them through the hall towards the front door.

Marfa Halaktionovna finishes her cup of coffee,

helps Yavdokha to put all the dried dishes away and finally sits down opposite the window. Her eyes wander far away in deep meditation. Beyond the garden's end she sees where wonderful horizons enchant the soul with a quiet yearning which does not stir one to rebel in the spirit of petty bourgeois impressionism, but, on the contrary, calms one down with the joyous peace of monumental realism.

Sometimes, Methody Kirilovich or Semen Yakovich (the chief director of the trust) may drop in at that time. Then, in the bedroom one can hear a discussion on such themes as "The Sex Problems in Our Society." However, it sometimes happens that nobody calls. Then Marfa Halaktionovna remains in her seat opposite the window reading "Jeanne Ney" until her husband comes back home, usually around five o'clock.

After supper my hero frequently attends a meeting. Sometimes, however, when there is no meeting, he rests on the sofa. On Saturday evenings Ivan Ivanovich goes with his wife and the family friend, Methody Kirilovich, to the movies. There he sees Soviet films. Ivan Ivanovich has no use for the theater. He likes movies, though only heroic war films at that or else pictures with a realistic and joyous content. They remind him of the days when he shed his blood for the Soviet republic, the day when the flaming Red Cavalry swept across the wide steppes of Zaporozhe. My hero hates satirical or traditional movies.

"There you are," he says if, by mistake, he happens to attend such a movie. "Again this petty bourgeois nonsense. It's strange. We live in such a wonderful

179

epoch, such heroic days, and there you have a pessimistic old tale."

"Well then, how do you explain the appearance of such a movie?" Methody Kirilovich sometimes asks, taking Marfa Halaktionovna by the hand. "What is the reason for it?"

Ivan Ivanovich takes off his glasses and wipes them with his snow-white handkerchief. "The reason is obvious," he replies carelessly. "A Marxist cannot fail to understand it."

"You are thinking, of course, of Plekhanov's formula?" Marfa Halaktionovna asks seriously.

"Of course," says Ivan Ivanovich. "Being determines consciousness. Besides, one must remember that our writers are a terribly backward lot."

"I entirely agree with you," says Methody Kirilovich and bids his friends good night.

Ivan Ivanovich and Marfa Halaktionovna now turn into Thomas More Street. A light autumn drizzle begins to fall. It sings plaintively in the gutters, and the petty bourgeois soul is overcome by anguish, telling man (to put it in plain language a la Stendhal) to rebel against the fact that in our society there is no room for satire—anguish which my charming hero, that most valuable citizen, Ivan Ivanovich, regards with such utter contempt.

However, there is no anguish or pessimism in Ivan Ivanovich's apartment. Brilliant electric light floods the room gaily, and May and Violet are smiling so happily. Here everything is pitched in a major key. It is so cosy and pleasant here in this revolutionary haven of peace that one really begins to wonder: "Good heavens, what else can we possibly want?"

At this moment Ivan Ivanovich comes up to the radio, makes a very simple movement with his hand and at once a beautiful symphony concert is heard. Isn't this a wonderful achievement of socialist construction? Take this very radio. Was it not for this that my hero shed his blood—in order that the proletariat might live in the fullest contentment, using all the means of modern technology?

It is true that some proletarians have not yet received their radios, but we must not forget the disgraceful conditions bequeathed by the old regime. Let us take the homeless, for instance. Of course, it is not pleasant for my hero to see these unhappy children. But what can he do? There is no room here for bourgeois philanthropy. One must make organized war on social evils. That's why Ivan Ivanovich never gives a penny to those individualist beggars.

May takes Violet's hand and waves "by-by" with it. He smiles happily and curiously at the radio. Mademoiselle Lucy smiles pleasantly too. So do Ivan Ivanovich and Marfa Halaktionovna. Yavdokha stands in the doorway and smiles. She smiles that joyous smile which shows that she has complete confidence in her masters and that she knows very well that any cook is a potential People's Commissar.

"Hop, hop," claps Ivan Ivanovich, "come on, Violet."

The candidate for the Octobrists suddenly waves so beautifully that everybody applauds.

"Ho la," cries out Mademoiselle Lucy. There is a strange cry outside the window and Marfa Halaktionovna thinks it is a siren of some sort. She looks out and cannot see anything but darkness. Rain is still beating against the leaves, but comrade Halakta pays no attention to it. She is thinking of the summer and is already planning how they (the whole family, that is) after a hectic year of work will be given a holiday and a reservation at a resort by their superior. Then once more they will see the beautiful Caucasus or the mountains of the Crimea. Then they will remember earlier holidays and their carefree laughter will echo among the mountains.

Finally, the children kiss their father's bald temples and go to bed. But before going to sleep they have to listen to materialist teachings delivered as a lesson in social education which most certainly has nothing to do with idealist bedtime-stories.

Marfa Halaktionovna lies down on the sofa. Ivan Ivanovich sits down and thus an evening of reminiscence begins, or perhaps a discussion on a contemporary theme, such as Communism and Socialism.

"It may sound strange," says Marfa Halaktionovna, "but I still do not understand what is the difference between Communism and Socialism?

"Really?" says my learned hero with surprise.

"Yes, for instance: what are we building today—Communism or Socialism?"

Ivan Ivanovich takes off his glasses and wipes them with his snow-white handkerchief. "Socialism, of course," says he confidently. "Communism is a higher stage."

"Such an answer does not satisfy me," says Marfa Halaktionovna. "Tell me simply—what are the concrete differences between Socialism and Communism?"

However, Ivan Ivanovich has no time to give a

concrete answer. The telephone rings. My hero picks up the receiver. He knows it is his friend Methody Kirilovich, they are going to have a nice long chat.

It is impossible to say how long this conversation will last. The reader can well imagine how Ivan Ivanovich goes on and on. So let's turn to a more interesting part of the story.

III

"Isn't it time for us to go to the meeting?" asked Ivan Ivanovich as the church bells started ringing for evening benediction.

Marfa Halaktionovna looked at her watch and agreed that it was time to go.

It was one of those Thursdays when each Party member of the communist cell to which Ivan Ivanovich belonged, participated in the construction of the first Soviet Republic in the world.

Ivan Ivanovich dressed first and then packed his briefcase. Marfa Halaktionovna also had to change. She put on an old suit and tied a simple red scarf round her head so that she might look modest and neat. When she dressed like this she reminded my hero of a factory worker in the tobacco plant. Ivan Ivanovich was also dressed modestly and more simply than on other occasions. His hat was definitely old and he even took an ancient military tunic out of the chest, a remnant from the days of War Communism.

There was something very moving in this changing of clothes, something that reminded one of the scene in front of the altar. But whereas the priest put on an ornate and "idealist" robe, in this case a better suit of clothes was discarded in favor of a simpler, more "materialist" dress, and all this was performed in an ordinary hallway. In a word, Ivan Ivanovich (Comrade Jean) and Marfa Halaktionovna (Comrade Halakta) were well aware of the transitory nature of the period in which they lived.

"You know," said Ivan Ivanovich, stepping along the asphalted Thomas More Street in his rubbers and carrying his old umbrella, "I have a wonderful idea."

"You always have wonderful ideas," said Marfa Halaktionovna.

Ivan Ivanovich looked a little confused, but he simply had to tell his wife his "wonderful idea."

"That socialism can be built in one country is a fact," he began. "This has been proved beyond doubt by Lenin and Stalin. However, if in our discussion, some people show their disbelief in it, one can, in my opinion, abandon this theoretical formula."

"What utter rubbish you are talking," exclaimed Marfa Halaktionovna, looking round to see whether, by chance, they had been overheard. "You must be careful, or else you will come right out with something like this one day. What would others think of you if they heard that you oppose the idea of socialism in one country?"

"That still won't make me change my mind," declared Ivan Ivanovich firmly. "Why do you want me to think in clichés? We are not against original ideas. I only wanted to point out that from this formula

184

one can make a slightly different one which would satisfy us and could not fail to satisfy the others."

Marfa Halaktionovna stopped walking and looked at her husband with surprise. "I don't understand you," she said.

"You don't understand? But look here," smiled my hero. "The whole crux of the matter is: are we building Socialism in one country alone? Well, are we?"

"I still don't understand you," repeated Marfa Halaktionovna.

Ivan Ivanovich looked over his glasses and said in a tremulous but happy voice, "What if, for the sake of argument, we pose this question: Russia—one, Ukraine—two, Georgia—three, Byelorussia—four. Are they all one country?"

"But you forgot the economics," interjected Marfa Halaktionovna.

"That's true; I didn't think of that. But such an explanation would be more acceptable to the masses," said Ivan Ivanovich.

"I see that your wonderful idea is just sheer stupidity," replied Marfa Halaktionovna sharply.

Comrade Jean felt a little offended; why should she be so outspoken?

"Nothing of the kind," he defended himself, "it is quite a good polemical approach."

"But your approach may lead you to accept a bourgeois Ukraine."

My hero suddenly slapped his thigh. Yes, that's quite right. He just hadn't thought of it.

Ivan Ivanovich, that is to say, was certain that "for the masses" we were building Socialism not in one country but in several. But because the press had always so far referred to Socialism in One Country, omitting all discussion of the matter, and because his own interpretation might be misunderstood by some people, he renounced his personal opinion and dutifully accepted the decision of the last plenum of the Central Committee. Thus, engaged in such an interesting conversation, my hero and heroine covered half the way to their destination, the path which, on Thursday evenings, was trod by members of the communist cell, gathering for their weekly meeting.

It was getting dark. Church bells were ringing and their sound might disturb the soul of every citizen. An ordinary citizen thought, of course, of Christ's resurrection. Not so Ivan Ivanovich. He tried to force himself to think of anti-religious propaganda. How grateful he would be if the factory sirens could be heard now. Then his soul (pardon me this inexcusable idealism—not his soul, but perhaps something else, something more monistic) would indeed be stirred. He would not think, then, about the primitive Christian commune but about materialist dialectics. This didn't mean, of course, that he would then simply attach a little Darwinism to some sociology. God forbid! If he really meant that, he would not have walked to the meeting hall all the way—*per pedes Apostolorum*—he would have taken a cab. All this proved again that, as Semen Yakovich once said, Ivan Ivanovich is and always will be an exemplary builder of the socialist state.

Soon, joined by Methody Kirilovich, Ivan Ivanovich and Marfa Halaktionovna entered the meeting hall of the communist cell.

186

IV

The room is pleasant and attractively decorated. Every corner of it reminds one that it is not just an ordinary corner, but above all, a "red corner." Nearly all the revolutionary leaders hang on the walls. Apart from these there are many revolutionary posters with various slogans—some of Trade Union, some of Komsomol, some of still other origin. The texts are so interesting, so beautifully and yet simply designed and so persuasive that one look at them is enough: everything becomes clear and obvious. On the right hangs the local wall newspaper framed in the monumental-realist style. It is a most readable newspaper. It has original contributions, like the one about "the little defects of the big machine," as well as sharp satires on the local bosses, like the one concerning the amorous escapades of the former Komsomol candidate, the girl machinist Popadko.

Ivan Ivanovich sat down on the nearest chair in the first row. Next to him sat his wife and Methody Kirilovich. It was very quiet. Occasionally a soft, restrained whispering could be heard here and there. The door squeaked as new arrivals kept coming in. Outside the church bells were ringing noisily and it seemed funny to think that across there, in the church, people were standing in front of candles, thinking about the "idealist" catacombs of the first Christian martyrs. Here were no candles; a purely "materialist" electric light flooded the room and the peole were not thinking any "idealist" balderdash.

"Can you remember what tonight's topic is?" Ivan Ivanovich softly asked his wife.

"Surely you haven't forgotten?" said Comrade Halakta. "Today's talk is on the latest assault upon self-criticism."

"Oh," said Ivan Ivanovich, holding up his snow-white finger.

He was right. His gesture meant that tonight he would listen most attentively to every word, that he would not fall peacefully asleep. This only happened when he felt that nothing very important was being said, and then he knew that at the right moment (when it was necessary to vote unanimously) his wife would wake him. He also knew that his communist cell would "never betray the interests of the proletariat."

"The topic sounds quite interesting," said my hero looking at Methody Kirilovich.

"Very interesting," agreed Methody Kirilovich and bending closer to his friend said in a subdued and mysterious voice, "we also have . . ."

"What?" asked Ivan Ivanovich.

Methody Kirilovich looked sharply round, to the left, to the right, to the rear, and then whispered clearly, "An obstructionist, a real heckler, guess where he is?"

Ivan Ivanovich, clearly surprised, sat back a little. "You don't say so?" he said, all agitated. "In our most exemplary cell—an obstructionist? Did you hear, Halakta?"

But Marfa Halaktionovna, having heard the sensational news, was already busy examining the faces of all those present. "Is it the courier?" she asked, fiercely scanning a distant figure sitting all alone in the last row.

"No," snapped Methody Kirilovich.

Marfa Halaktionovna again let her eyes race across the room. By now the cell gathered, so to speak, *in corpore*. All the members of the Collegium were there. Also present were all the heads of sections, all the chiefs and their assistants from the various bureaus, the head of the local Trade Unions with three officials, the head of the Communist Women's Organization with her two secretaries, and the wife of the local Communist Party chief, who like Marfa Halaktionovna, had no special post because, like Marfa Halaktionovna, she devoted her time to bringing up her children. Only the secretary and the chief, who was to deliver the talk, were still absent.

Comrade Halakta was still trying unsuccessfully to guess who the obstructionist was. "Perhaps it is that cleaning woman," suggested Ivan Ivanovich.

"Out of the question," said Methody Kirilovich. "She can't be an obstuctionist, as she is only a candidate for the Party."

"Who on earth can it be? Please, don't tantalize us any longer, Comrade Methody," almost pleaded Marfa Halaktionovna.

Methody Kirilovich felt indeed that, as a communist, he had no right to tantalize his comrades any longer. Looking sideways, he said ironically, "There he is—Comrade Leiter."

Marfa Halaktionovna fixed her eyes on the small figure of Comrade Leiter who sat far to the left. "Yes," she said with a sigh, "yes, that's quite possible. He may be an obstructionist. Have you noticed his face, Jean? How very pale and, I would say, degenerate it is. I always suspected that he was an anarchist-individualist."

"You may well think that he has picked up some ideas somewhere," said Methody Kirilovich with his eyes wandering over the floor. "Nothing of the kind. Your own man, so to speak. That's why it is so strange."

"What do you mean by this?" asked Ivan Ivanovich rather naively.

"Well, it doesn't matter," said Methody Kirilovich waving his hand.

However, this mysterious reference to "your own man" intrigued Marfa Halaktionovna, although she understood the hint. "Why do you always keep hinting at things?" she asked. "Why 'your own'?"

"Never mind. To tell you the truth," said Methody Kirilovich, "I am really sorry for Comrade Leiter. His behavior will give our anti-semites a pretext: once again they can point to a Jew acting against the Party."

Methody Kirilovich began to tell then how deeply shocked he had always been by anti-semitism (for instance the Beyliss affair) and how much he liked the Jews. Moreover, he believed that the Jewish nation had produced the greatest men in history. "Let's take Christ, for instance," he said. "Our people don't even know that Christ was a Jew."

"And where is he working now?" asked Ivan Ivanovich.

"Who—Christ?" Methody Kirilovich looked surprised.

"No—Comrade Leiter, of course."

My hero put on another pair of glasses and observed

the obstructionist curiously. That Comrade Leiter was a Jew was of no importance to Ivan Ivanovich. Social struggle knows no national barriers. However, Ivan Ivanovich, as a devoted Party member, must condemn anyone who opposes self-criticism and the Party program for the proletariat. When Ivan Ivanovich now learned that Comrade was in charge of the trust's library he thought: a member of the intelligentsia and a demoralized Party member.

By now Comrade Leiter had attracted the eyes of nearly everybody in the room. Marfa Halaktionovna told the news to her neighbor, her neighbor passed it on to her neighbor and so on. The looks centering on Comrade Leiter were so penetrating that his pallor seemed to increase.

At last the church bells stopped ringing. Benediction had begun. Into the room came the chairman and the secretary of the cell. Everything was quiet, even the whispers died down. Everybody was tense with expectation. The discipline of the cell was exemplary and all the members respected and honored their chief.

"Comrades," said the secretary stepping on to the podium. "May I have the nominations for chairman of this meeting?"

"Semen Yakovich," called out several voices.

The chief (Semen Yakovich) adjusted his tie, smiled pleasantly and waving his hand declined the honor. "Thank you, a thousand times thank you for your confidence, but I simply cannot."

He pointed to his throat and so the public thought that he found the room too stuffy. They also knew that the Chief's heart was not too good. However, both these guesses were at once dispelled by the secretary.

"Semen Yakovich cannot be in the chair, as he himself is going to deliver the talk," the secretary informed them.

"Ah—that's something quite different," some voices were heard. The cell, bearing in mind the Party's directive about the middle-rank democracy, suggested somebody from below.

"Methody Kirilovich," said a few.

Ivan Ivanovich felt a strange sensation under his heart. The point was that he and Methody Kirilovich had, so to speak, equal rank: both were members of the Collegium and both were regarded as next in importance to the chief. That is why my hero felt rather odd and thought it must be just another misunderstanding whenever the cell nominated Methody Kirilovich.

Marfa Halaktionovna thought, however, that it was quite right to nominate Methody Kirilovich. "Naturally," said she, "one has to give a chance to those who are not at the very top. Semen Yakovich and yourself cannot always take the chair." She said this to her husband after Methody Kirilovich had left her side and, upon a unanimous vote, had taken his place as chairman of the meeting. Ivan Ivanovich was grateful to his wife and calmed down a little.

"Comrades," said Methody Kirilovich, "the first item on tonight's agenda is a talk on the latest assault upon self-criticism." The speaker is Semen Yakovich."

Dead silence fiilled the room. One could even hear the autumn drizzle beating against the windows.

Some listeners looked at their chief who rose to speak and placed a copy of "Pravda" in front of him. Some looked at Comrade Leiter who cracked his fingers and looked down on the floor.

"Comrades," the chief began, "my last talk was about the necessity of economizing. What did I say? I said that we, the communists, cannot remain indifferent to the program of economizing. What is meant by economizing? Economizing is one of the latest slogans of our proletarian Party and one has to understand it, not only in its wide interpretation, but also to find a place for it in our private lives. Let's take the pencil as an example. How would we regard it if there were no 'economizing' slogan? Well, we would regard it, so to speak, with indifference. I myself had the honor to see how one of our comrades (here Semen Yakovich smiled pleasantly looking at a certain member of the executive) threw away a pencil which was not yet completely used. Yes, ha, ha!"

The chief halted for a moment, poured himself some water and, after drinking a glassful, looked with a fatherly but scolding eye at the member of the executive who had thrown away the pencil not yet wholly used. The entire auditorium also looked in that direction. But nobody's glance was evil; everyone smiled though perhaps with a hint of scolding, like the chief. All knew that the member of the executive just referred to was a fully enlightened member and that he would not do it again.

"Well now," continued Semen Yakovich, "what should have been done in this case to observe the economizing slogan? Well? Of course, the pencil should not have been thrown away. A holder should have been purchased at the price of two kopeks and then it should have been used until the very end. That, in my opinion, illustrates economizing in everyday life."

The speaker drank another glass of water and continued. "And now I come to the topic 'the latest assault upon self-criticism.' What do I see there? I see in it the same lack of realization. By this, I do not want to offend our esteemed Comrade, Klimenty Stepanovich, and compare his error with the pencil to the illegal opposition to self-criticism, but the elements of poor consciousness are, so to speak, the same in both situations."

"Semen Yakovich," interrupted the member of the executive, "I admitted my mistake long ago. In Party matters I have no personal ambition."

"Splendid," said the chief, "in Party matters there can be no personal ambition. One always had to admit one's mistakes publicly and openly. But let us return to the subject. Well now, 'the latest assault upon self-criticism'."

Here the speaker assumed a serious expression, pulled out a pair of pince-nez and spread *Pravda* in front of him. Then, dutifully and without any lyrical digression, he read to his cell the article on the value of self-criticism, an article to be read and listened to by all Party members, and thus to be heard by all here. The talk was highly interesting, the audience responsive as they had rarely been before.

"Now let me sum up," said the chief at last. "So the latest assault against self-criticism is, so to speak, an entirely stupid and bandit-like act. We firmly believe that it will never succeed (here Semen Yakovich's face became very menacing) ; the proletariat, comrades, will force the issue!"

Loud applause followed the chief's speech. Somebody called out "Long live our leaders!" The audience almost rose to its feet to sing the International. Such enthusiasm hadn't been seen in the cell for a long time. One felt that in the face of a threat from Comrade Leiter, the proletarian avantgarde had presented a firm and united front.

"Comrades," asked Methody Kirilovich when the audience calmed down a little. "Are there any questions?"

Everybody turned to look at Comrade Leiter. Surely he was going to speak? No matter how difficult it might be to speak against such a united body, there was no other way out for him.

"May I say a few words?" asked Comrade Leiter at last.

The audience stirred and then quietened down. It was just like the moment before a storm, when the trees are still before an approaching typhoon. One could hear the autumn drizzle beating against the windowpanes and Ivan Ivanovich wiping his glasses with a snow-white handkerchief.

"Comrades," said Comrade Leiter. "Not only have I no desire to criticize the decisions of the Central Committee of the Party, but on the contrary. . . ."

However, the typhoon struck. The audience stirred.—Just listen, what arrogance! "He has no desire to criticize the decisions of the Central Committee." That's what we have come to! What a nerve! A mere nobody—and such pretentiousness. Did you hear? "He has no desire to criticize the decisions of the Central Committee." What impudence!

"Comrades," called out Comrade Leiter, paler than before. "Allow me to express some thoughts on the real problems of self-criticism."

What—what does he say? "Real problem of self-criticism." What a scholar! Where did he get all this wisdom all of a sudden? What arrogance! How selfish! That's enough! We cannot tolerate demagogues like that!

"Comrades," Comrade Leiter called out once more. "I only wish to say a few words about the members of our cell."

The audience began to rage. Each member felt the fighting spirit of an old Bolshevik surging up in his breast. Everybody was about to get up and shout: Enough of that! We don't want any Menshevik sermons!

"Comrades," Comrade Leiter tried for the last time, "I . . . I . . . we . . . we . . ."

But in vain. The typhoon raged furiously. Methody Kirilovich made a sign with his hand and the typhoon vanished. Methody Kirilovich turned to Comrade Leiter with a fatherly smile.

"As you see, Comrade Leiter, the audience does not want to hear you. I can't help it. Your ideas simply do not find any response."

Comrade Leiter cast down his eyes (of course, he was sorry to hear that his ideas found no response) and sat down.

"Who else wants to speak?" asked Methody Kirilovich.

Ivan Ivanovich realized that his turn had come.

He must get up and display his rhetorical skill in the struggle against the local opposition.

"May I?" he said and victoriously walked up to the speaker's desk. My hero took his briefcase, placed it on top of his chief's, wiped his glasses with a snow-white handkerchief and began.

"Dear Comrades! Our Comrade Leiter wants to play the part of a missionary. He wants to preach what you recognized as doubtful and alien ideas in this country—the country that never was Christian. *Episcopus in partibus!* You understand?"

Here Ivan Ivanovich, like his chief, poured himself a glass of water and looked at the audience from above his glasses, as if saying: Well—not a bad introduction?

"Clever," several voices were heard.

"However," continued my hero, "we have no time for such missionaries (voices: right, quite right!). Comrade Leiter spoke a great deal assuring you that self-criticism was a waste of time, that self-criticism will halt our economic development, and so on and so forth. However, I say to you—nothing of the kind! It can never halt our economic progress (voices: quite right!). Who believes in what Comrade Leiter has just said? Who does?"

"Nobody," shouted several.

"That's right. Nobody. Absolutely nobody! (Here my hero let himself go.) We all remember how dearly we paid for the establishment of the dictatorship of the proletariat, how we shed blood on the battlefields in the civil war, how many of our comrades were executed by the enemy. We cannot remain silent. We must tell Comrade Leiter to keep his hands off the proletariat and not to try to turn our heads. He would like to split the Party, but he will fail. He will . . . enough . . . enough . . ."

Here Ivan Ivanovich clutched his chest and said that he could not finish his speech because of his weak heart. His address was rewarded by stormy applause. It was clear now that Comrade Leiter had met with utter failure. The cell remained loyal and united.

There were other speakers after Ivan Ivanovich, but they had nothing new to say. Everything was clear, and so Methody Kirilovich closed the meeting.

Cell members were going out into the street. It had stopped raining. Heavy clouds still hung over the city.

"Well, how was my speech? All right?" asked Ivan Ivanovich.

"You spoke beautifully," said Marfa Halaktionovna. "Maria Ivanovna was enthusiastic about you."

"It is a pity my heart won't let me do it right through," sighed Ivan Ivanovich. "But you know, I am convinced that I am a born orator."

V

My hero and heroine were back in their apartment. Here everything was in perfect order. Yavdokha was washing up, Mademoiselle was embroidering a shirt for her future fiancé. The children were peacefully asleep.

"You don't remember if any notes were passed to me during the meeting?" asked Ivan Ivanovich.

"I don't think so," said Marfa Halaktionovna.

My hero, who was in a very contented mood, put own his cup of tea and took out his briefcase. "Well, 1 any case let's have a look. Perhaps I was so excited hat I didn't notice. Some people might have passed ome notes to me." Ivan Ivanovich began to search is bag. Then all of a sudden he took out a document nd laid it on the table. "What on earth is this?" he sked and turned pale.

"What have you found?" asked Marfa Halaktio-ovna.

Ivan Ivanovich looked distractedly at his wife and anded her a document. Marfa Halaktionovna saw he papers marked "secret" and also turned pale. "I on't understand it," she said.

"I wonder if someone planted it in my bag on pur-ose—to compromise me? What do you think?"

Marfa Halaktionovna looked carefully at the ceil-1g. She was thinking. At last she spoke.

"Everything is possible. You have many enemies."

"What's that, many enemies? Halaktochka, I have 1any enemies? You never told me this before!"

"I didn't want to worry you," sighed Marfa Halak-ionovna. "You have a weak heart, so there was no 2nse in telling you about it before."

"Who are these enemies?" cried out Ivan Ivano-ich.

"I don't know," sighed Marfa Halaktionovna. How can I know them, if they hide themselves?"

Ivan Ivanovich, in his despair, tore at his hair and ent over the table.

And yet Ivan Ivanovich was right. The document hich someone had put into his bag was dynamite. It was a record, perhaps legal, but not yet published of minutes of the plenum of the Central Committee. In fact, it was almost a whole booklet, perhaps quite secret, perhaps not; my hero had no time to read it now.

Just then the autumn drizzle became more audible behind the window and for a moment Ivan Ivanovich thought that, who knows, there may be experiences in life that are definitely in a minor key and that the bright electric light may sometimes shine, not joyously and confidently, but somehow differently.

"Well, what shall we do?" he asked in an agonized voice.

"We must burn this document at once, that's all," said Marfa Halaktionovna.

"Burn? Are you sure that's the best thing to do? What if they planted it on purpose in my bag and then ask me what I did with it? Perhaps I should take it back to Semen Yakovich?"

"If you keep it," said Marfa Halaktionovna, "they may ask you where you got it from, which is worse."

"God, what shall I do?" groaned Ivan Ivanovich.

Marfa Halaktionovna did not know what to do either. She was turning in her mind all the possibilities, yet the cursed document glared from the table and so far there was no solution. At last, however, Marfa Halaktionovna brightened up and said, "I know; it's a misunderstanding."

"What do you mean?" asked Ivan Ivanovich hopefully.

"Tell me where was your briefcase? Wasn't it on top of Semen Yakovich's bag?" she asked.

Ivan Ivanovich put one finger to his lip and thought. "Yes, I think it was," said he after a while.

"Now it's clear. Listen! Semen Yakovich himself must have put this document into your bag, and he must have done it by mistake."

"How by mistake?" Ivan Ivanovich could not understand.

"I remember that he took something out of his bag. It must have been this secret booklet. He probably wanted to quote from it during his talk. Later he must have changed his mind, and of course by mistake he put it into your bag instead of into his own," explained Marfa Halaktionovna.

"How very clever!" cried out Ivan Ivanovich. "Darling, you are a real Sherlock Holmes. But how shall I ask him about it?"

"Oh, that's simple," said Marfa Halaktionovna. "Call him up and ask him if he has lost anything from his bag."

My hero leapt up from his chair and ran to his study. He could be heard lifting the receiver and saying clearly: 4002. Engaged? Damn it! Then again, 4002; what still engaged? At last, however, he got through to Semen Yakovich. Two minutes later my hero was back in the dining room.

"You were right," he called out, embracing his clever wife. "You were absolutely right. Semen Yakovich put the document into my briefcase by mistake."

Marfa Halaktionovna was very pleased too that all had ended well and suggested that Ivan Ivanovich should have a glass of Armenian vodka before his supper.

* * *

Ivan Ivanovich was lying down on his "surprise" mattress, reading the latest issue of *Pravda*. From the radio came the music of some light opera and from the kitchen the sound of Yavdokha washing up. May and Violet were peacefully asleep. Marfa Halaktionovna undressed and jumped into the "surprise" bed, pushing her husband right up against the wall with her formidable torso.

"You still haven't told me what is the real difference between Socialism and Communism," she demanded of her husband.

"Really?" said Ivan Ivanovich. "I've already told you. Communism is a higher, an ideal stage of social development."

Marfa Halaktionovna yawned and turned off the light. In a moment both comrades could be heard snoring peacefully. The autumn drizzle was still beating against the windowpanes, but not in a minor key; on the contrary, everything seemed to be happily settled. Sound asleep after the tragic incident with the document, Ivan Ivanovich dreamt of the quiet fields and soft sky, where wonderful horizons enchant the soul with a quiet yearning that doesn't stir one to rebel in the spirit of petty bourgeois impressionism, but, on the contrary, calms one with the joyous peace of monumental realism.

VI

How then shall I end this story? Alas, not with Ivan Ivanovich's dream (let him sleep peacefully!) but with a description of the tragic catastrophe which so suddenly overtook my innocent hero, so devoted to the cause.

First of all, my hero's invention forces me to add another short chapter, although an impatient reader may skip it.

After autumn comes winter. The frost was severe, but my hero was very busy in his warm apartment in Thomas More Street. The house in which Ivan Ivanovich lived was competing with a house in Shchukin Street. In this "socialist contest" each house tried to show how best to use fuel. Thus the contest was not only against the bourgeoisie, but against the forces of nature.

One day, sitting in his overheated apartment, Ivan Ivanovich said to Marfa Halaktionovna: "You know, I feel that I can serve the Party most of all by carrying on my Party and social work, and secondly, by inventing something.'

"What have you in mind, Jean?" asked Marfa Halaktionovna, eating nuts which were sent to her as a gift by her brother, a forester in a state forest. Marfa would not touch nuts produced privately. "Tell me all about it," she encouraged Ivan Ivanovich.

"You see," he said, "I was just thinking about the summer. When it comes we shall have flies again. You know how much they hinder our work. They are a real nuisance. So I have decided to invent a fly-killer. I shall invent one—you will see. On my communist word of honor, I shall. You think I lack the talent?"

"Why, no," said Marfa Halaktionovna, looking up at the ceiling. "I have no doubt about it. Sometimes one finds talent even among the simple folk, and you, certainly, are a person with a higher education."

Such a response from his wife to his desire to invent a fly-killer encouraged my hero so much that he started work at once. First of all, he wrote a letter to his cell asking to be relieved of his ordinary duties because of the great burden of his own work. Next day he received a reply relieving him of his duties because of "research work conducted for the purpose of scientific invention." Then Ivan Ivanovich began to work on his fly-killer.

In a short time Ivan Ivanovich became, as he put it, "the hero of our time." He succeeded in inventing an electric fly-killer. His fame spread everywhere, and Marfa Halaktionovna was even prouder of her husband than before. The construction of the gadget was kept secret, but it was known that the fly-killer was very efficient in electrocuting flies which happened to settle on one particular part of the instrument.

"The only snag is," said Ivan Ivanovich, "that flies do not always sit where I want them. Well, it doesn't matter," he added.

He was quite right to add that it didn't matter. The main thing is to make a start. That's what my hero had done. Later, others, perhaps his own son, May, will perfect the invention. Ivan Ivanovich was satisfied.

* * *

After Christmas Comrade Misty (a pseudonym), a brother of Marfa Halaktionovna, came to visit Ivan Ivanovich and his family. He was the forester who sent nuts to Marfa Halaktionovna. He came to stay for an indefinite period of time since, as it turned out, he had been excluded from the Party and relieved of his duties as a forester. Evil tongues had it that he was expelled for dishonesty, but Comrade Halakta maintained that this happened because of Misty's "opposition" and "deviations."

Ivan Ivanovich had no time for deviationists. However, in this case he could not "fight the opposition," not because Misty was his brother-in-law, but because my hero was a noble and tactful person and could not offend his guest. "To fight the opposition" was all the more impossible since very disturbing rumours about "some changes in the Politbureau" began to circulate just then.

Comrade Misty whole days lashed out against the "bureaucrats" and assured Ivan Ivanovich that "they won't get away with it this time." Ivan Ivanovich listened carefully to all this while Marfa Halaktionovna talked.

"I think," she said " that Zuzia is right in what he says about the 'bureaucrats'. What do you think, Jean? Certainly I always had a grudge against Stalin."

"I have nothing against it, Halakta dear," sighed my hero, "as to Stalin, I agree with you (here my hero looked carefully around). You are quite right. In my opinion, he is, so to speak, an obstructionist. Let's hope he will meet with an obstructionist's fate."

"Let's hope," shouted Comrade Misty.

All this did not mean, of course, that my hero was beginning to turn tail at the last moment. He was simply saying that in this question also he could not help being an "out-and-out revolutionary," and that all he wanted was the complete victory of the proletariat, so that one could go to one's cell on Thursdays and live in peace during the rest of the week. He had suffered enough in the wars.

"And yet," Comrade Misty pestered them, "please tell me what you think of this idiotic idea of self-criticism?"

Ivan Ivanovich took out his snow-white handkerchief and nervously wiped his glasses. Of course, he knew how he should answer such questions, but Comrade Halakta was the first to speak. Making sure that the door was shut she said in a conspiratory tone:

"Of course, Jean, all this is absurd. Surely you don't believe in self-criticism now? Tell me."

Ivan Ivanovich was a firm believer in self-criticism, but when he heard that Comrade Halakta did not agree with the idea, he found it difficult to defend his belief, all the more because Comrade Misty assured him that the "Party bureaurats" who were in favor of self-criticism were about to be purged and lose their power.

"No, I don't agree," he said decisively and, encouraged by a kind look from his wife, my hero added that even from the start he had had little faith in the idea of self-criticism. In a word, all the time Ivan Ivanovich was saying what was dictated to to him by his revolutionary consciousness.

However, Comrade Misty changed his view on self-criticism as soon as he landed a new job. Ivan Ivanovich then felt that he had to defend his old view; he began to propagate forcefully the idea of self-criticism. This only showed that my hero, being an orthodox Marxist, could not help wielding expertly the weapon of materialist dialectics. Therefore it was all the more strange that this great tragedy, this grand catastrophe could have happened to my hero. My last chapter is devoted to it.

VII

One day Ivan Ivanovich was lying down after a lunch reading the *News*. He always read this newspaper carefully. First of all he found here all the official decrees, and my hero wanted to be versed in the course of events shaping socialist construction. Secondly, Ivan Ivanovich liked the paper for its contents. The *News* had everything: humorous sketches, articles on co-operatives and land problems, and on cultural life throughout the country. Most of all Ivan Ivanovich liked the editorials, especially the ones that were never signed.

"No matter what you say," he kept repeating to his wife, "this paper should be an example to our local newspapers. What beauty of expression! What an amount of stimulus for the heart and mind in these editorials! How varied and exciting the topics! This is how a paper should be edited!"

"No wonder," sighed Marfa Halaktionovna, "this is our oldest newspaper. Soon it will have had ten years of experience."

Ivan Ivanovich looked out of the window and saw that snow was falling gently. His soul was filled with joy and pride ...

One day, later, Ivan Ivanovich was lying down on

the sofa after a very good lunch reading the *News*. Suddenly his eyes dilated and he grew pale just as he did when he found the secret document in his bag. His fingers began to tremble. To make matters worse, there was nobody at home. The whole family had gone to a public park; there was only Yavdokha left in the kitchen. Ivan Ivanovich rubbed his eyes and once more read carefully the lines which had given him such a shock. Then he got up and started to pace up and down the room. He was very upset and excited. One would think that any news which could upset him must be that of war at least, or perhaps of the enemy forces already advancing against the Soviet republic, or the unexpected death of one of his beloved Soviet leaders.

"Betrayal of the Revolution," he murmured. "Clear betrayal. Unless the paper is lying? But I always believed in it. If it's not lying, then . . . No! It can't be true! No! . . ."

Ivan Ivanovich felt cold sweat on his forehead. He felt as if he would collapse and, like a wounded hare, sink down on his "surprise" carpet.

However, thank God this didn't happen. My hero slowly calmed down and at last regained full control of himself. He walked up to the window and opened it wide. Outside it smelled already of early spring. The sun was just setting. It was setting peacefully as if nothing had happened. Its ball of fire looked perfectly indifferent. Ivan Ivanovich did not pay any attention to it. What did he care about the setting sun! He was back to normal, anyhow. True, his hands trembled a little, but he could not help it. He wiped the sweat off and not having anybody with whom to share his worry, he suddenly felt a great desire to talk to his cook.

"Are you washing up, Yavdokha?" he asked in a soft, caressing voice, stopping on the threshold of the kitchen. "How are you getting on? Do you like it here with us?"

"It's not bad, Sir," answered the cook (see how ungrateful they can be), "I got used to it.'

At any other time my hero would not have noticed the offensive "sir!" Comrade Halakta even thought that it was all right for a cook to call her master "sir," because in any case nobody hears her, and besides a cook should never be deprived of the liberty of using words she prefers. This time, however, Ivan Ivanovich reacted very sharply.

"What 'sir' am I to you, Yavdokha?" he shouted in obvious despair. "What are you saying? I am no 'sir' to you." Here Ivan Ivanovich smiled and added, "comrade, yes, that's what you should call me, comrade!"

Yavdokha looked at her master with obvious surprise. "I don't mind if you prefer it that way," she said shrugging her shoulders and taking up the pail of dirty water.

Here something quite unexpected happened to my hero. Almost jumping, he drew nearer to the cook and seized the pail from her. "Yes, yes, Yavdokha," he said in a trembling voice, "I am no 'sir' to you. I am your friend and comrade. I have always told you to call me 'comrade'."

It is true that Ivan Ivanovich didn't himself believe that he had told Yavdokha to call him 'comrade', but he didn't believe it not because he never did such a thing, but because he might have forgotten about it.

Ivan Ivanovich again wiped off the sweat and said: "Allow me, I'll take the pail out."

The last phrase simply escaped from my hero's lips. But once out, it could not return (for a word is not like a fly; you can't catch it, not even with a fly-catcher). Ivan Ivanovich felt that he was performing a heroic deed, but Yavdokha refused to let him carry the bucket. A tussle developed. It is impossible to know how all this would have ended, for at this moment the door opened and Marfa Halaktionovna appeared on the door-step.

"Jean, what on earth are you doing?" she said curtly, observing the struggle. "What is the meaning of all this?"

Comrade Halakta misunderstood the whole scene, of course, thinking that my hero was flirting with the cook. Without hesitation she turned to Yavdokha: "Get out!" she shouted, "get out this moment! And don't let me see you here again!"

"Oh, what are you doing, Halakta?" pleaded Ivan Ivanovich. "Please, don't, darling. I implore you!"

However, Marfa Halaktionovna did not pay the slightest attention and kept shouting "Get out!" When the cook finally left the kitchen and Ivan Ivanovich, all wet with perspiration, took his wife by the hand and led her to the sofa, she didn't let him speak for quite a while. She raged. She was hysterical. At last, when Marfa Halaktionovna fell exhausted on the sofa, her husband had a chance to explain everything. My hero managed to persuade his wife that he was not flirting wtih Yavdokha, but simply helping her to carry out the bucket of dishwater and so to show her that there is really no difference between him and a cook. It was at the moment when Marfa Halaktionovna ceased to doubt her husband's faithfulness that her eye caught the fateful lines in the *News*. However, with the help of eau de Cologne she controlled herself this time.

"Please, don't get excited, Jean," she said calmly. "Don't panic; I don't think the members of the Collegium will be purged."

"Ah, my dear," said my hero in a resigned voice, "you haven't read it all. Read to the end." He held the paper before her. "Please, look here, it says that the purge will include even the members of the Central Committee of the Communist Party. Yes, even the members of the Central Committee."

"This is impossible. I don't believe it," declared Marfa Halaktionovna. "They can't purge the members of the Central Committee. This would mean the betrayal of the Revolution."

"That's exactly what I said. Betrayal of the Revolution." Ivan Ivanovich in deep despair was holding his head in his hands. "What are they up to? After all, I was right to disagree with self-criticism. Now I just can't trust the leaders, that's what it had come to. I give you my communist word of honor: I just can't trust them."

Then, still very excited, Ivan Ivanovich walked over to his study and telephoned Methody Kirilovich. "Have you heard the news? Yes, sure! What about you? Please, come round tonight. We must have a family council."

That night Ivan Ivanovich and Marfa Halaktionovna could not sleep. In the morning my hero hurried to the office. He even forgot to kiss May and Violet on his way out. In the office he met with an even greater disappointment. He was told that he would be affected by the purge (it seemed that his favorite paper was right as always). Secondly, he learned that a special commission would investigate the activities of his communist cell. Methody Kirilovich told him about it.

"Why a special commission? Why an investigation?" asked Ivan Ivanovich feebly, quite pale after a sleepless night. "Tell me what is the purpose of it all?"

"Well, they just want to purge somebody, that's all," said Methody Kirilovich. "And not only somebody from the cell—but somebody from the presidium as well."

"From the presidium?" asked Ivan Ivanovich in utter despair (after all, he was a member of it). "What are you saying, Methody Kirilovich? You are just being panicky. You are wrong, yes, you are. I can't understand how it all started."

"If you want to know, just ask your Comrade Leiter," added Methody Kirilovich. "I bet you it's all his work."

"Why did you say 'your Comrade Leiter'? What do you mean by it?" asked Ivan Ivanovich who for a moment forgot all about the glasses he was wiping with a snow-white handkerchief.

"Yes," said Methody Kirilovich calmly, "your Comrade Leiter. I am not a member of the presidium, but you are. You should have known what Leiter is made of. Why, I told you, but you didn't do anything about it."

"Now, I don't understand anything," said my hero in utter resignation.

Later my hero went to see the chief of the communist cell and the chairman of the presidium, Semen Yakovich. I don't know what they talked about. Perhaps it is better so, for the details of my hero's tragic downfall might be too painful to narrate.

What finally happened was this. A special commision investigated the cell and found that Comrade Leiter was not a wrecker or bandit, but a devoted Communist. Secondly, the presidium of the cell was reorganized (this must have been a tragic misunderstanding). Thirdly, Ivan Ivanovich, Marfa Halaktionovna, and Methody Kirilovich were obliged, as they put it, "to leave the Party."

* * *

Ivan Ivanovich came back home after the purge and wept like a child, bent over his fly-killer. Suddenly everything seemed to him to be pitched in a minor key.

"I am lost," he said to himself, "God, what a tragic misunderstanding. Why should I, of all the others, suffer so much for the cause of the Revolution? What have I done wrong?"

His last question remained unanswered. Marfa Halaktionovna was not at home. May and Violet had gone for a walk with Mademoiselle Lucy, and Yavdokha did not know and did not much care what had happened. She was singing in the kitchen—an odd song, which although in a major key, irritated my hero very much.

213

And so we have come to the end of this story. I can see some disappointed faces among my readers who will tell me that this is not literature, but cheap journalism.

I can't help it, dear readers. All I want is that my story should be read by all the citizens of our republic, and, as you know, most of our citizens read cheap journalism, not literature. Therefore, I have to make a compromise.

And remember, please, Thackeray's opinion of Swift (remember "Gulliver's Travels") —that so great a man he seemed that thinking of him was like thinking of an empire falling. Ivan Ivanovich agreed with this at one time, and today I share his views when I reflect on the work of the bitter English satirist.

———

Translated by G. and M. Luckyj.

HIS SECRET[1]
(Reminiscences)

ARKADY LYUBCHENKO

Somewhere from out of the Don steppes a strong wind was blowing, rushing into the Kharkiv suburbs and down along the streets until, hemmed in and roaring like a hurricane, it reached the central square in front of the Executive Committee building. But the circuitous snow flurries which seemed at times almost like a blizzard were winter's final fling. The snow was melting as soon as it touched the ground, and the black asphalt square was wet and blotchy with puddles.

I was hurriedly making my way through the crowds of pedestrians struggling against the wind. My collar turned up, my hat pulled down over my eyes, I was sunk within myself, indifferent to all. Suddenly the wind struck me full in the face, forcing me to turn sideways and shield behind my shoulder. At that moment I felt a jolt forcible enough to stop me. I

[1] This, somewhat abridged, is a translation of Lyubchenko's "Yoho tayemnytsya" published in *Nashi dni* (May, 1943).

was angrily trying to spot whoever might have pushed me with such impudence when, unexpectedly, a pair of large, glowing dark eyes regarded me very closely. A golden sparkle shone in them. The eyelids quivered and the eyes themselves narrowed while around them, in the dark sockets, nests of darting wrinkles formed. These were tired, yet warm and smiling eyes.

"Well, go on, swear at me, Arkadeo," a hoarse bass voice was heard from behind the upstanding collar.

"Devilish wind," I remarked, expressing both my anger and surprise.

"The cursed wind," agreed Khvylovy; and without changing his cocky, boyish attitude he ended by reciting a line from Tychyna's poem.

I love none like the wind.

"I can see that, old man. I think this love is pushing you on like a dray-cart."

"And you, old man, are forging ahead like a steam engine. Ha! So you see, we did quarrel after all. Now we shall feel better. By the way, you are in love with the wind too, but then you mustn't only love it while you are sitting over your desk. It is interesting that our modern literature is so preoccupied with the wind. Have you noticed? There are scores of examples. Why is this?"

"The elements attract many."

"May be. But why should it be exactly this element that attracts them? Don't you think that the wind is a symbol of the force and zest with which we began the revolution? This, and a lot of other things too. This belongs to the past. Don't you think that now it symbolizes another factor—the peculiar

216

anguish? Yes, it is an expression of this awakened and insatiable longing. Do you see? This element represents an awakened force, an urge, a flight, and then a crash . . . the raging steppes, the boundless horizons . . . the incredible distance beyond. Distance is always tormenting. Just as if a man suddenly felt that he had wings, tried to spread them, and found that they had gone. Do you understand? Not a predestined fall like that in the Russian verse about the 'windmill which waves its wings but cannot leave the earth,' not hopelessness. On the contrary, an urge to fly up, a passionate striving and faith. Yes, the yearning for something which is possible, realizable, although very, very distant."

Our conversation was carried on under most unfavorable circumstances. Our breath froze in the icy wind, our lips were taut, and the words broke up and were lost. We moved to one side to avoid the crowd, stooping to shelter from the snow storm.

Mykola was small in stature, but sinewy and assured. He was continually wrapping himself in his worn black overcoat. His familiar threadbare black cap sat askew on his head. He would thrust it on carelessly, and then forget it altogether, giving his friends a chance to tease him. He wore a hat only for a very short period. That was after his return from abroad. Soon afterwards, however, he gave it up and returned to his old, so much more comfortable cap.

Under the felt peak one could clearly see his thick, eagle's eyebrows which were very mobile. His swarthy face, marked by a few prominent lines, became darker and thinner in the cold. Yet it preserved a youthful look, and shone with a debonair daring and pugnacity. Only the corners of his mouth sometimes hinted at a stubbornness which was perceptible in the short, determined chin.

However, Khvylovy's most striking feature was his eyes. They were large and deep, like forest lakes.

"Where have you come from and where are you going, Arkasha?" he asked, twitching his shoulders and touching the tip of his nose with his fingers, as if chasing away a fly.

"From the editorial office—in fact, from several of them. Getting ready to take a trip into the country."

"To the country?"

"Yes, I have just been given an official recommendation and so I shall be able to move more freely and look into the most obscure corners."

"Yes, yes, and of course you will write."

"Well, I shall have to satisfy the editor somehow. But for myself . . . I cannot let such an opportunity go. I must learn with my own eyes what is happening in the villages, where the root of all evil lies, what are the reasons for this catastrophe, this black spring, and finally how all this is likely to end!"

Khvylovy looked downcast. He took me by the arm and pulled me aside.

It was the spring of 1933, the memorable year of the famine. The Central Committee of the Communist Party, expressing in a purely bureaucratic manner its sympathy with the starving and suffering people, accused these very same people of causing the famine. The entire propaganda apparatus of the Party was working tirelessly to demonstrate that peasant conservatism allegedly stood in the way of the introduction of new collective methods of farming; it stirred up the destructive elements. The *kulaks* were chiefly to blame. Saboteurs and wreckers, enemies of the people, the Ukrainian nationalists, who wanted to create confusion among the toiling people, to arouse opposition to the Soviet government, and to exploit this in order to fulfill their 'counter-revolutionary' schemes were also guilty. This argument was persistently and universally applied and was illustrated by fresh examples every day. The Bolshevik propagandists in this demonstrated all their skill and talent, which were considerable.

Under the weight of 'evidence' and under the influence of clever political swindling, the public began to lose their ability to discern events clearly and to judge them accurately. Many people, of course, had their doubts about the explanations being offered; they suspected that something suspicious was hidden behind the nervous agitation. The doubts multiplied. People wanted to get at the facts, to tear off the veil of propaganda and to touch the truth.

"It's strange," said Mykola, "you have beaten me to it by only a few minutes. I was just on my way to the editorial office with the very same intention."

Without releasing my arm he led me in the direction opposite to the one in which I was going, towards the editorial office. I followed him mechanically. As if confirming our intention he stressed once more: "Yes. We must see it for ourselves." Then he asked me where exactly I was thinking of going.

"At first, perhaps, into the Lokhvytsya district. I will visit Bychok at his sugar refinery, and then go to some of the villages."

"That's a good idea, to see Bychok," Mykola replied, "by the way, Vasylkivsky is now the secretary of the district committee in Lokhvytsya."

"I know. The one who used to be the secretary of the Kharkiv Locomotive Works, and fell out of favor."

"Yes. He may be helpful. He is a good man and a fine Ukrainian patriot."

We left the square and were walking in the old quarter of the city, through its narrow, crooked streets and alleys. It was more sheltered here and we both felt some relief from the wind

"Listen, Mykola, what if you come along too?"

"This time I am ahead of you. Yesterday I sent a note to Bychok telling him that I might call on him within the next few days," said Khvylovy, smiling triumphantly, with a gay gleam in his eyes.

"Well, that's splendid," I said, unable to hide my delight, "so we are going together."

His bushy eyebrows drew together, and his face assumed a serious expression. "No," he said calmly, "that, unfortunately, is impossible. I'll be in your way."

"What the blazes, how can you say such a thing?" I grew angry, though I knew very well that Khvylovy was always careful not to disturb other people's work. I told him that each of us would be able to do what he wanted without interfering with the other, that it would be much better for us to be together, especially under the present complicated conditions. Finally, I asked if I should be in his way—that would be different.

"No, not one bit," replied Khvylovy emphatically, "but you got the editor's recommendation first."

"And you were the first to let Bychok know. That settles it. We are going together."

"Very well," he said, "I will call you tonight."

I held out my hand to seal the bargain with him. Just then a third hand, long, yellow, and trembling like a leaf, reached out to us. Its numb fingers were stiff with cold. Softly an imploring voice was heard: "Take pity, not on me, but on my children."

It was a young woman, grown prematurely old with grief. Her dress and speech betrayed at once that she was a peasant. Beside her stood her two little boys, dressed in clumsy clothes, blue with cold and terrified by the city.

Every day hungry peasants such as these could be seen in the city. The authorities had ordered them to be kept out of the capital, but in vain. Somehow they managed to find their way into the city and they swarmed through the old quarters. The militiamen pursued them brutally in the streets, but it was impossible to catch all of them. Stealthily they moved along sidestreet and alley. They lacked the technique of professional beggars and therefore often begged mutely, with a silent gesture or look. The woman who stood before us with outstretched hand bore herself proudly; her hand looked unnatural, as if it were that of a stranger. Only her eyes burned with intense suffering.

Khvylovy drew out his purse, turned it inside out and gave all his money to the woman. I did the same. The woman bowed, astonished, and moved away. Her sons, bewildered and hungry, trotted after her, hanging on to her coat.

"She, above all, is entitled to bread, since she helps

221

to produce it," said Khvylovy in a somber voice, "and yet she has to beg for a piece of bread under socialism."

He was looking at the crowd, among whom the woman could still be seen, and helplessly he swung his clenched fist through the air. He wanted to say something, but checked himself. Through his tightly-clenched teeth there emerged the crisp line—

I love none like the wind.

Its bypaths and its anguish, I continued.

Mykola looked once more in the direction of the crowd into which the woman had melted and, deep in thought, he shook my hand.

————

We lived in Barrack Lane, in the large new apartment house for writers which bore the high-falutin name *Word.* Although our quarters were quite comfortable, to live in this 'gilded cage' under compulsion was difficult to bear. Writers who constantly met each other in editorial offices, publishing firms, clubs, and perpetual obligatory meetings, commissions, debates, conferences, and plenums, who therefore often hated the sight of each other and belonged to different literary circles, were forced to live under the same roof, as if in a barrack. Even in their homes they could not feel free. Every step, every movement could easily be watched by one of the neighbors, whose voices could be heard through the walls. So in this impressive-looking building nearly everyone walked on tiptoe and talked in a whisper.

Ever since the great purge of Ukrainian writers

had started, the building was under constant surveillance by the NKVD, whose stooping agents could be seen prowling around it. They would sometimes come inside to search for 'counter-revolutionary' evidence, to rip up walls and floors in the hope of finding it there. The inmates of *Word* were seen burning and destroying their papers and letters, and often they were taken away, never to return to the clean and sunny rooms, and their families were heard moaning and crying. It was then that our apartment house came to be known as the "crematorium."

Khvylovy lived on the third floor of the "crematorium." Having recognized my steps, he was waiting just inside the open door. He wore an old hunting outfit, large gumboots, a greasy military uniform and a faded leather jerkin, a relic of the civil war. He showed me in and offered me a drink, which I refused. Then he excused himself, saying that he had to finish packing his rucksack.

His wife then motioned to me from the next room. When I approached her, she carefully closed the door and whispered: "I am so glad that you are going with Mykola. He is in a terrible state. Please look after him, restrain him."

She was in deep distress, wringing her hands, and only just able to control the tears which flooded her eyes. She was a thin, pale, gentle woman who, during the revolution, fought at her husband's side against Denikin. Later, the revolutionary ardor subsided and, disillusioned with the regime, she left the Party. Now she stood there, worn and prematurely aged, and assured me in a worried tone:

"Something is going to happen, mark my words.

Mykola threw out a strange hint. And you know how right this terrible intuition of his is."

I tried to calm her, and assured her that I would take care of her husband during the coming journey.

"Well," said Khvylovy ironically, "we are going to study a new and most important phase of socialist construction—the famine. We shall see what help we can offer. Where is my *casquette*?" he asked his wife, purposely using the name given to his inevitable cap by his friends. It was obvious, however, that his gaiety was assumed and that underneath there smoldered a burning disappointment.

———

Only through the good offices of an old friend of ours who worked at the station were we able to secure a compartment on the train, which was stormed by crowds of waiting passengers. They were extremely agitated, pushing their way blindly; fighting and trampling each other, losing their relatives, screaming and swearing, animated by one desire: to get into a carriage. The train was jammed and as it moved away, hundreds of those who had failed to board it made a last desperate attempt to secure a foothold on the outside. Some fell off and were crushed under the wheels.

Khvylovy's pallid face was as impenetrable as a mask. Silently he lay down, looking at the ceiling. I sat down in a corner of our compartment. We remained silent until the conductor came. Punching our tickets he looked carefully at Khvylovy and said: "I think I must have met you somewhere before."

"Quite possible," replied Khvylovy.

"And you, too, remind me of someone," he turned to me.

"Really?" I said, annoyed by his talkative behavior. However, he assured us that he had spent many years wandering among the passengers and involuntarily remembered some faces.

Soon afterwards a trainman came to sweep up our compartment. He also talked a great deal, complaining against his superiors, and cursing the people who littered and soiled the carriage.

"It's not their fault," I interjected.

"That's true," he eagerly agreed with me, "such rioting is going on everywhere. I wonder what it will all end in? To tell you the truth, it's the government which is to blame."

We remained silent. Looking up at the upper bunk where Khvylovy was lying motionless, the trainman turned the handle and was about to leave. Yet his desire to talk proved stronger. He started grumbling again and shrewdly led up to a direct accusation against the government.

"I can see that you are conscious . . ." I began.

"Yes, of course," he replied.

"A conscious counter-revolutionary," I ended my sentence.

The trainman was petrified. His face was now truly comical. Khvylovy started to laugh out loud, so loudly that I could not restrain myself from following suit.

"I see you are joking," said the trainman finally, forcing a smile. "But you should not joke like this with anyone. Especially when I was openhearted with you."

"So was I," was my reply. "If you had not been conscious, I would have argued with you, trying to persuade you. But I see that you are a conscious comrade, perhaps even a Party member."

"Party or non-Party, what does that matter?" he defended himself, "But I am half-illiterate, and you are educated. And you agreed with my errors, didn't you? Which of us is the counter-revolutionary, then?"

"Whoever comes out," I said to him and quickly opening the door I showed him out. The trainman became confused, taken aback by a new surprise. "Please," he stammered.

"No, that's enough," I said firmly and closed the door behind him.

Khvylovy was still laughing. "What a rat!" he said. "However did you have the patience to talk to him for so long?"

"Well, we have seen another significant product of socialist construction."

At last we could talk. We talked about the shameful system of state security which made one half of the population watch over the other half. We talked about the "Russian dungeon of peoples," about the stuffy Muscovite interior, now being covered with a red *sarafan* though of the same Ryazan-Tambov make. We talked about the blind alley into which the Revolution had entered, about the bourgeois mentality and the complete pathological degeneration of the leading communist stratum—how completely incapable it was of realizing the basic needs of social justice and universal progress. We talked, about the absolute inevitability of the new "Thermidor." We talked, too, of the intimidated and derided Ukrainian people with a talented but half-decimated, half-bewildered and wholly disunited intelligentsia. We argued passionately, disagreed, and fell into reveries while the wheels rumbled monotonously and the train sped on.

Our compartment was filled with cigarette smoke. I went out and stood on the platform. My head was burning, and the cool air which flowed from the steppe through the broken window was very refreshing. The train came to a halt at a signal. In the stillness of the night one could hear the bitter sobbing of a child. Lower down, on the platform, next to the buffers, I could discern the shapes of people. I asked who was crying. A man explained that it was a little boy who had apparently lost his father. I made my way down to where sat the sobbing child, among five others. He fiercely resisted all my attempts to take him into the warm compartment. Only after prolonged coaxing did I succeed in moving him from his place.

Khvylovy gave the little boy a warm welcome, and at once offered him something to eat. Our little snub-nosed guest continued to nestle, looking around warily and scowling like a little wolf. Yet Mykola soon succeeded in putting him at ease. We learnt that the little boy had lost touch with his father and the rest of the family at one of the stations where they were all attempting to push their way into the carriage. The mention of his father again brought tears to the eyes of the child.

"You just wait, snub-nose," said Khvylovy, "we shall look for your father. Don't worry, we'll find him," he assured him, and before I could say anything, he had disappeared from the compartment.

How surprised and delighted we were when, after some time, Khvylovy reappeared with the father. He had searched all the carriages and finally had discovered a man who had lost his son. Now the family was once more happily reunited. Besides the father there were also two daughters. Our compartment was just big enough for all of us. The little boy joyfully snuggled against his father who stroked his head with his rough hand. The elderly peasant told us of his bitter lot. He said that on his farm he had fulfilled all the quotas required by the state, then had scraped the last scrapes to meet the additional quota, only to be asked to give more. Where could he find any more grain, if he had nothing to eat himself? His wife had died and he was left with three children. Many in his village had perished from famine, and therefore he had decided to move down to Podillia, to a relative of his; perhaps life was more bearable there.

The door opened and the trainman came in. "No admittance to outsiders," he said sternly to our guests, and added, "Come on, get out of here."

We protested, declaring that they would only travel with us as far as Romodan, and that they were there at our invitation.

"I repeat: no admittance to outsiders!" the trainman haughtily enunciated, citing the regulations of the train.

Khvylovy hunched his shoulders, got up, and asked the trainman to have some regard for the poor, tired people. He also offered to pay the difference for their compartment seats.

"I tell you once more, 'no admittance to outsiders' —get out of here!"

Khvylovy jumped up like lightning. He seized the trainman by the arm. His face was aflame, his eyes were wild and his lips were white. His entire body was poised for a savage blow.

"You cad, don't you dare! Get out! And don't you show yourself as long as I am here!"

The trainman slipped out. We didn't see him again.

At Romodan we helped our guests to buy tickets for another train and shared some of our food with them. Stepping over hundreds of sleeping people, we finally reached the platform where we had to wait for our train to Lokhvytsya. From almost the end of the platform stretched the wide steppe. Everything was still, and the lighted station looked like a lonely, enchanted ship in the dark sea of the steppe. Before us lay the fabulously rich Poltava soil, where the people were dying of starvation.

In the morning we got out at the first station after Lokhvytsya. Here a new Stalin Sugar Refinery had been built two years ago by Czech engineers, a factory famous throughout the USSR. Its director was an experienced worker, formerly a sailor in the Black Sea fleet, a man of iron physique and clear mind, with great organizing ability. He was our friend, Bychok. We had met him on our earlier visit to Lokhvytsya. Bychok gave us a warm welcome. Next day Vasylkivsky arrived from Lokhvytsya. Both men told us much of what was happening in the district. Apparently the peasants were showing open opposition to the government. State property had been destroyed, government officials had been murdered. The reprisals which followed were met by even stronger opposition and armed rebellions in the villages. The food situation was desperate. Famine was so widespread and severe that there were cases of cannibalism. The government was at a loss what to do—whether to punish the transgressions by public execution, or whether to keep them dark for fear of further uprisings. Officials were confused, orders from above contradicted each other. Chaos was staved off only by means of intensified terror.

We wondered whether all this was the inevitable byproduct of collectivization. Our hosts disagreed; they argued that mass destruction and human sacrifices could have been avoided if conditions had been properly studied beforehand, and all the difficulties had been taken into account. They called the present policy 'dynamiting,' which, in effect, turned the Ukraine into a blazing volcano. Was it possible that the men in the Kremlin, who had planned this policy were fools? Of course not. In that case they had made some errors. Or were the local executives responsible for the chaos? No matter where the blame was put the general direction of this policy was impossible to explain. It was aimed at uprooting, weakening and destroying the whole population.

Clasping his head with both hands, Khvylovy listened to all this very attentively. He was extremely agitated. Pacing up and down he suddenly stopped, declaring: "Comrades, once more I am going to say something 'against the stream.' I shall again commit a 'heresy.' This famine is an organized job. It had been created to provoke the resistance and, in crushing it, settle once and for all the dangerous Ukrainian problem. This First Five-Year plan of Stalin is only the third act of the drama. Two more acts still await us. Shall we all have the patience to see the play through? Will there be anyone courageous enough to call: Enough, curtain!"

———————

In a few days we set out to visit some of the villages. The carriage moved slowly along the muddy road, and it was already growing dark by the time we finally approached the village of Hamaliyivka. To our left, in the distance, one could see a hamlet and in the fields in front of it people were raking the soaked soil. The coachman explained that they were searching for last year's grain which, although rotten and bitter, was still eatable.

"Spring is here, the peasant is triumphant," Khvylovy ironically quoted Pushkin.

Noticing that he was boiling with rage, I recalled the following line of Horace, in order to restrain him a little:

> *When life is hard keep calm,*
> *And in good times refrain*
> *From insolent rejoicing*

Mykola was silent, his head bent down. Then, as if shaking off the black thoughts, he added:

For, Dellius, you cannot escape death.

In the calm steppe evening, the hooves of the horses squeaked noisily in the gluey mud and the wheels of the carriage grated in agony. The road, cut in several places by the railroad, which was under water, shimmered with a reddish light. The setting sun burned the edges of huge clouds which cast a grey and golden dust over the whole sky. There was something almost apocalyptic in this view.

"Is one afraid to die?" asked Khvylovy, "What do you think?"

"That depends on circumstances," I replied, "I have faced death on several occasions, but had no time to be afraid, because I wanted passionately to live."

"Yes, that's when death comes unexpectedly. But if it doesn't," he continued, bending towards me, "I think that one must be afraid to die: let's admit this."

Having said this, Khvylovy became fidgety, flicking his nose with two fingers as if to chase off a fly.

———————

The village soviet of Hamaliyivka had been notified of our arrival by telephone. We were taken to the spacious house of a peasant who had a large orchard. Our host had scarcely greeted us when he started to enquire about government measures to deal with the famine. Industrious and stubborn, he had managed to keep himself and his family alive, and even possessed a cow. He slept in the stable with this most precious possession, barricaded and armed to the teeth, ready to fight for it if necessary. He told us that the village was almost completely deserted. Later in the evening, when we went out, we could see not a single light in any of the houses. It was ominously quiet. Even the cats and dogs had all been eaten up. Before us lay a cemetery.

On one of the following days I was quite unexpectedly taken ill. Khvylovy did everything to help me. He telephoned the doctor and asked him to come quickly. However, the roads had become quite impassable and our village was a veritable island. Not until four days later did the doctor arrive from Lokhvytsya and diagnose typhus. I tried to take the news calmly, and at least knowing what it was I felt that I had a chance of pulling through, provided I received proper treatment. Khvylovy was genuinely alarmed and nursed me until I was taken to a hospital in Lokhvytsya. He accompanied me to the hospital, and decided to return to Kharkiv in order to find a bed for me in one of the hospitals there.

Before he left I asked him to come closer to my bed.

"Listen, Mykola," I said, "Typhus is a long, tiresome business. In case anything should happen to me, will you . . ."

"So you are afraid, after all," he said, "and remember how brave you were, talking about it. Listen, Arkasha. What right have you to die? Who told you you can die? Nobody. I am telling you: you must be prepared to live. To die, my friend, is the easiest way out. Anybody can do it. But to live—that's something worth trying. To live and to struggle—especially now; that's highly praiseworthy.

"It's true, in certain rare cases death is better, when through death perhaps one can do more for one's fellow men than by living. But such cases are rare. . . . Today, we must first of all fight for physical preservation. This is our most important task. And I ask you to fulfill this task. Do you understand? To live, at any price."

His words fell deep into my heart. They fortified me and I had now no doubt that I would live.

"You must live," said Mykola, bending down, "because there is something else I have to tell you. It's a secret. I cannot tell you now, but I shall, as soon as you recover."

This was at the end of April; two weeks later Khvylovy shot himself.
